Typewriter Pub, an imprint of Blvnp Incorporated
A Nevada Corporation
1887 Whitney Mesa DR #2002
Henderson, NV 89014
www.typewriterpub.com/info@typewriterpub.com

ISBN: 978-1-64434-147-6

DISCLAIMER

This book is a work of fiction. The characters, incidents, and dialogue are
drawn from the author's imagination and are not to be construed as real.
While references might be made to actual historical events or existing
locations, the names, characters, places, and incidents are either products
of the author's imagination or are used fictitiously, and any resemblance to
actual persons living or dead, business establishments, events or locales is
entirely coincidental.

HOW TO SAVE
A BAD BOY

KAIRY AGUAYO

type
writer
pub

For Isaiah,
My little U.S. Marine. A story you encouraged to write based on our
adventures.
This one is for you. I'll be right here when you come back.

PROLOGUE

MORGAN COLLINS

You know that angsty teen in your school? The boy with tattoos? The one who started sh*t for absolutely no reason? You know, the bad boy? Every school had one. You either knew him, had an unpleasant interaction with him, or heard about him at least once.

Whichever it was, you probably wanted nothing to do with him.

I had never really bothered talking to the bad boy in my school mainly because he skipped class most of the time.

Until today.

"I need your help." He was obviously drunk, and I was obviously confused.

"What the fu—" Mason pushed a hand to my mouth and looked at me with wide eyes, almost as if he was afraid to be heard.

"Shhh. Someone is gonna hear us, Maddy. I-I need you to be really quiet, Maddy," he slurred as he tossed his leather jacket to the side. I furrowed my eyebrows at him. To be honest, I had no idea who Maddy was and I also didn't know what Mason Hunter was doing in my room this late at night or how he managed to get in.

Actually, now that I was thinking about it, how did he know where my room was? Did he just choose randomly? If so,

1

what would have happened if he had chosen my mom's room? I shook my head, scolding myself for overthinking. It probably wasn't even that deep.

"I'm going to let go. Promise you won't scream?" He giggled when I nodded and carefully removed his hand.

I hissed at him. "What the f*ck are you doing here?" He looked rather attractive even in the darkness of my room. Tousled brown hair, big golden eyes, and a jawline that could grate cheese. *Yummy, cheese. I should try to test that theory.*

Mason giggled once again and shushed me. "You don't swear, Maddy. You're a good girl."

I rolled my eyes at him and let out a breath. "What are you doing here?" I asked again, a bit irritated with his current state.

"I'm running from the c-cops." He chuckled as his eyelids started to flutter. "I beat up a guy," he whispered the last part as if there were a lot of people who might hear him. My eyes widened and I looked at him in disbelief. I suddenly turned my focus on his clothes, which were stained red.

"Mason!" I called out, hoping to catch his attention.

"Shhh, don't scream." His eyes closed completely as he passed out on my carpeted floor; mine widened further as I stared in horror. There were red splotches all over his white shirt. I hoped it was Kool-Aid.

His jeans were torn, and nope, it wasn't Kool-Aid.

I turned to look at the alarm clock and nearly cried out in despair. It was 3 AM. What would my parents do if they found a delinquent in my room at this hour? Not just any delinquent, a f*cking bloodstained delinquent.

"Screw me," I hissed as I further inspected his torn jeans. I couldn't really see a lot, but I could tell he had an open cut. I washed my hands, then retrieved the first aid kit from my restroom. I then sat next to Mason's unconscious body.

I can just let him bleed out.

2

Shaking my head at the idea, I unbuckled his jeans and hesitantly pulled them down to his knees.

"This is wrong in so many ways," I muttered as I caught sight of his underwear. Good thing he was unconscious or this would have been very awkward for the both of us.

I bit my lip as I saw the gash on his thigh. With shaky hands, I wiped the crusted blood off his leg and applied antibacterial ointment on the cut. I then reached for the bandages.

Mason hiccuped. "If you wanted to get in my pants, you could have just said so." I snapped up. He watched me mischievously with his golden eyes. Mason was quite the casanova, which wasn't a surprise considering his looks. He had a sharp jaw, high cheekbones, and a perfect strong nose. Although it was his confidence that really got the girls.

I pushed his head back down slowly and continued working. I did not bother to say anything. I could feel my face burn with embarrassment.

He chuckled and picked his head back up, observing every detail. "Don't worry, Maddy. I probably won't remember this tomorrow." I sighed when I heard his low snore and shook my head. *This can't be happening.*

CHAPTER ONE
Don't Punch Him in the Face

By the time morning came, Mason was already gone. The rest of that morning sailed on quickly, and before I knew it, I found myself sitting next to my best friend during lunch.

Dee raised her dark brow at me as she shook her head. "Girl, I knew you had a few screws missing when I met you, but I didn't know that it was this bad."

I hissed as I fiddled with the food on my plate. "I'm being serious, Dee. He was in my room."

Dee scoffed and turned to look at Mason, who was sitting alone with his head down. "You want me to believe that that hot piece of ass sat in your room last night?" I nodded and took a note from my pocket that had a messy handwriting sprawled all over it.

"I don't know when he left but look."

Thanks, Maddy
-M.

"Who the heck is Maddy?" Dee questioned as she took the paper in her hands. "And why does he have such a messy handwriting?"

"I don't know, Dee. That doesn't matter," I groaned as I threw my hands up for effect. Dee shook her head and set the paper down, grabbing onto my hand. She smiled apathetically.

"Honey . . ." she trailed off. "I know you're all riled up, but there's no need to make up stories. There is no way Mason freaking

Hunter was in your room last night because he was too busy getting it on at Richard's party."

I ripped my hand away from hers and stood up. "I'll prove it," I stated stubbornly. Before Dee could utter another word, I darted towards Mason's table and sat next to him. I could feel the stares of the other students at the back of my neck. Not everyone had the f*cking balls to approach Mason when he was in a sh*tty mood.

"M-Mason," I said shakily, then cleared my throat. I repeated myself with a more confident tone. "Mason."

His head shot up, revealing a pair of sunglasses. He probably had a bad hangover judging by his physique—messy hair, clenched jaw, and bruised knuckles. He wasn't having a good day, and I wasn't making it any better.

"You left your jacket at my house."

I expected him to smile at me after last night. "Who the f*ck are you?"

I looked at him in disbelief and felt anger coursing through my veins. *I wish I actually threw him out of the window.*

"I—"

He sighed. "Look, if I had sex with you last night, don't get the wrong idea. I have sex with everyone. It doesn't mean we're dating."

My mouth fell open and I searched for the right words to say. What could I say in response to that? "No, you didn't. You don't remember anything?"

He lowered his sunglasses and narrowed his eyes. "If I remembered, I still wouldn't be here playing charades with you."

I hissed through gritted teeth as I clenched my fist. "I have your jacket." This boy made my blood boil.

"Do you have it right now?" He raised his dark brow.

I shook my head. He rolled his eyes, adjusting his sunglasses on the bridge of his nose. "Then stop wasting my f*cking time."

Before I could realize what I was doing, my hand flew past me and straight to his face. The cafeteria grew quiet as I drew my aching hand back. His sunglasses flew off his face. He slowly advanced towards me, his golden eyes bore into my dull green ones.

"Run, b*tch, run!" I heard Dee curse from the other side of the cafeteria.

Mason had never hit a girl, but he also had never been assaulted by one, so who knew how he would react! His face neared mine until it was a few centimeters away. His eyes flashed with anger, but his lips quirked up to a sarcastic smile.

"Get the f*ck out of my face."

Don't need to tell me twice.

I lurched up at his words and stumbled to run to the other direction.

He was going to assassinate and screw me. I was too young. There were so many things that I needed to do like . . . Okay, I couldn't think of anything right now, but I was pretty sure I had a bright future ahead of me.

Maybe not, but I still want to live!

"Girl . . ." Dee trailed off.

"I know," I simply responded.

*   *   *

Later that night, I found myself awakened by the sound of my window clicking shut. I searched frantically for the sound. My blood ran cold when I caught sight of Mason sitting on my windowsill with a cigarette in his hand.

I need to call the cops. I need to scream for help. I need—

"You should really lock your windows. I'm sure you don't want a psychopath breaking into your house."

Maybe if I just jump out the window . . .

Mason stood up and kneeled next to my bed. He reeked of cigarettes, soap, and alcohol.

6

"Don't hurt me, please," I murmured as I inched away from him. "I'm sorry I hit you. I didn't mean to—"

"Don't worry, Maddy. I'm not going to hurt you." He smirked as he put out his cancer stick on my nightstand. "Not physically anyway."

Wait, what?

I turned to look at my alarm clock and winced at the time, *11 PM.*

"Then why are you here?"

He smirked boyishly and inched his face closer. My heart sped up as he halted dangerously close to my face, our noses were touching.

I instinctively closed my eyes, waiting for him to close the space.

Then he was gone.

"I came here to get my jacket," he stated as he took the leather jacket from the chair positioned next to my desk.

I stared at him dumbfounded, no doubt my cheeks were flushed. Did I really close my eyes? What kind of a f*cking idiot was I?

I heard my window open again. "And Maddy, please lock your f*cking window."

I stared at him as he began to climb out of the window gracefully as if he had done it many times before.

"My name's Morgan, assh*le."

CHAPTER TWO
Don't Tell Him What to Do

"You know, you're strange," I murmured as I sat next to Mason in anatomy class.

"What do you want from me?" Mason groaned and adjusted his sunglasses, clearly annoyed at my interest in our friendship. I huffed and snatched the sunglasses off his face. If he was mad before, you should see his face now.

"You should really stop drinking so much." I shrugged and placed the glasses on the table.

Mason furrowed his brows. He was looking at me as if I had just grown a second head. "You literally punched me yesterday, and you're here sitting with me? Can you give any less sh*ts?"

"If it would make you feel any better, I f*cked up my thumb when I punched you," I muttered, glancing at my right hand with a pout. Anger flashed past his face, and he reached to grab my wrist with a tight grip.

"If you don't leave now, I'm going to get charged for assault and I don't think either of us wants that."

I should have left and never turned back. I should have listened to him. Unfortunately for Mason, I was a really stubborn person. It was a gift and a curse. After I saw a challenge, I would stop at nothing to achieve my goal and Mason was being a very big challenge at the moment.

"Nah, I think I'm fine here."

"What the f*ck did I do to make you think I am your friend?" Mason growled in frustration and slumped back, signaling his defeat.

I raised a brow at him. "Do you not remember going to my house last night?" *And the night before that?*

He rubbed his face with his hand and rolled his eyes but didn't answer my question.

How can he not remember? How drunk was he?

"I'm not your friend," he admitted bluntly and looked at my paper. "Morgan? What kind of name is that?"

I glared at him to which he responded with a shrug. "Whatever. I don't need to know. Don't talk to me again and please don't tell me what to f*cking do." He gathered his stuff.

"Or else what?" I challenged with a raised brow.

I was so f*cking stupid, I know. This was the guy who had been in and out of juvie since he was fourteen years old, but here I was, annoying the sh*t out of him.

He wrapped his fingers around my arm and pulled me up, ushering me towards the door.

"Morgan! Mason!" Mrs. Porter exclaimed as she watched us leave.

Mason flipped her off before slamming the door, which earned a fit of giggles from the classroom.

"Where are we going? We're going to get in trouble," I murmured as I tried to pry his fingers off my arm.

He hissed. "I'm showing you what happens when you don't leave me alone." He led me out the doors of the main building. I furrowed my eyebrows and opened my mouth to speak but was rudely cut off by Mason. His golden eyes flashed with mischief as his plump lips stretched out into a smirk.

"Have fun, f*ckface," he said before shoving me into the janitor's closet and slamming the door shut.

I felt panic course through my body as I stared wide-eyed at the door. He wasn't going to leave me here . . . right?

I started to knock on the door frantically, hoping he would have a change of heart. "Mason, you can't just leave me here!"

"Or else what?" he mocked. I was honestly surprised he was still there.

"Or I'll . . . I'll kick your ass!" I pushed at the door once more and it finally opened, revealing a very amused Mason.

"Okay. Kick my ass then," he murmured as his eyes twinkled with amusement. For once, there was a taunting smile placed on his face.

I took a fighting stance and positioned my fists in front of me, causing him to snort. "Like this," he said as he reached out towards my fist. He was adjusting my thumb. "If you do it the other way, you can break your thumb. How do you not know that?"

"Not everyone grew up throwing rounds with other kids." I scoffed as I felt my face turn red. Mason rolled his eyes but nodded, waiting for the blow.

Is this guy f*cking nuts?

I landed a hit on his shoulder, and he rolled his eyes again.

"Come on, f*ckface. You can't possibly be that weak."

My arms fell and I narrowed my eyes into slits. "At least I don't lock people in closets when I'm pissed," I hissed under my breath. Mason raised his eyebrows and started taking steps forward.

"Do you want to go back in the closet?"

My eyes widened and I quickly raised my hands in surrender. "No, no, I'm good."

Mason put his hand on his chin as if he was pondering the issue, then shrugged. "I think you do."

Before I knew it, he pushed me in the closet again, then I heard a click.

I froze. "What was that?"

"Me locking the closet," Mason answered casually from the other side. I jiggled the handle and stared at it in agony as I realized he was telling the truth.

10

"How'd you get a key?"

I could imagine him shrugging and licking his lips as he said, "I stole them from the janitor."

"Mason . . ." I trailed off warningly. "Get me the f*ck out of here."

"I don't think I will," he taunted as I started hearing fading footsteps.

"Mason!" I exclaimed. I waited for a response and slumped down when I heard nothing. I searched the room for anything that could help me escape the situation but failed. The only thing that I could do was scream my heart out in hopes that someone would call the janitor. However, I doubt anybody had extra copies of the key. The school was so underfunded that it refused to buy or do anything that would waste money. Last year, Mr. Torres lost his key, so he had to open the classroom with a hanger for the remainder of the year.

The bell rang and I almost shed a tear at how lucky I was. The hall was soon filled with endless chatter and footsteps.

"Hello?" I exclaimed as I banged on the door. "My dumbass is locked in here. Can anybody call the janitor or literally anyone else?"

"Hello?" a male voice responded. "Who is this?"

I held the urge to groan in desperation. *Why the f*ck does it matter who I am?* "Morgan," I answered.

"Collins? The weird girl from calculus?" the voice questioned. I threw my head back as a response.

"No, Morgan Freeman. Get some f*cking help," I growled.

"Not with that attitude." The boy scoffed and my head popped up quickly.

"Look, I'm sorry. I'm just having a bad day, and I appreciate you answering my call. Can you just please get someone to help me out?" I pleaded.

"Fine. I'll be right back," he responded. I threw my hands up in the air to celebrate. *Yeah, that's right. I don't need Mason to help me get out of the closet.*

Mason: 1

Morgan: 1

"Morgan," Mrs. Vanderwall, the principal, called out. "We're going to get you out of there. The fire department is on its way."

I almost had a heart attack at her words. *The whole ass fire department? Can't we just pull up Mr. Torres's hanger?*

"Morgan, did you hear me?" Mrs. Vanderwall asked.

"The whole ass fire department?" I voiced out my thoughts and heard her gasp from the other end.

"Language!" she scolded and I rolled my eyes. My vocabulary was the last thing to worry about right now.

"The entire ass facility of people who combats fires?" I tried again. I could just imagine her debating if she should just leave me in the closet.

"Yes, Morgan. Mr. Right can't find his keys anywhere, and I don't have access to a copy," she explained in an annoyed tone and it was almost in a scream.

"Okay," I said lowly as I took a seat on the floor, feeling defeated.

"How did you get stuck in there?" she asked and I racked my brain for any explanation. I couldn't snitch Mason out; nobody liked a tattletale. So what could I even tell her?

"Um, I thought it was the restroom?" I said, although it sounded more like a question.

There was a long pause before she answered, "Morgan, are you stoned?"

"No, I'm not high!" I exclaimed. "I just got a little confused with the location of the restrooms." I narrowed my eyes with disgust as the words left my mouth. I really was stupid.

"Excuse me, miss. We need you to back away from the door," I heard another voice chime in. I did as I was told.

It didn't take them long to bust the door open. A group of students had circled the closet, and in the very front was Mason twirling the keys on his forefinger with a smirk on his face.

Mason: 2

Morgan: 1

I wasn't snitching on Mason. No. I was going to get even.

CHAPTER THREE
Touch His Dingaling

I tugged at the hem of my dress as I shook my head at Dee. "I don't know. I look extremely slutty. Plus, I wasn't even invited."

Dee snorted as she parked in front of a house. "You look fine," she reassured.

My stomach churned with nerves as I watched teens scattered across the lawn of Richard's house, which was huge! Richard Venice had always been the one to host parties, usually when his parents were away. Dee always attended but I never bothered.

Dee's eyes softened and she turned her body towards me. "Look, babe, Troy always came with me to these and I just want to show him that I can still be a baddie without him. I don't want to look like a total loner and who else am I going to bring besides the most beautiful and understanding girl I know?"

"Don't oversell it." I narrowed my eyes at her. She was trying to use her recent break up to get me to pity her. I wasn't buying it.

"M, we're already here and Mason will be here too. That means you can get to plot your revenge on him!"

I sighed, rubbing my temples in distress. Revenge? On Mason? It was a stupid idea. How could I get a revenge on him?

"Fine," I murmured, "but we're only staying for an hour and a half."

"That's my b*tch," Dee squealed in delight as she opened her car door. "Let's go."

I struggled to walk towards Richard's door in the stripper heels Dee owned but managed to make it without any broken ankles.

"This music is too loud!" I exclaimed as my ears were literally murdered by a song I couldn't quite remember the name of.

"That f*cker!" she exclaimed as her face suddenly contorted into a snarl. "He's already with another girl."

Before I could say anything, she pulled in a random guy and started making out with him. I thought his name was John or something. I was really bad with names.

"I guess I'll go for some drinks," I said awkwardly and started backing away slowly. Dee just gave me a thumbs up but didn't let go of the guy. I caught a glance of Mason with Lacey Earl, a nice preppy cheerleader with long red hair.

I knew what everyone was thinking, "Morgan, you stupid piece of sh*t, don't go near Mason. Don't do it, you slut. It'll only get you in trouble."

But who else could I talk to? The only people I was friends with was Dee and her ex-boyfriend. Other than that, I was friendless. I also wasn't too keen on watching Dee make out with what's his face.

"Hey!" I greeted and sat down next to Mason on the sofa. He looked straight up bored before I got here, but now he looked extremely annoyed.

"Of course you'd be here," he groaned as he took another swig of his drink.

Lacey smiled brightly and jumped up in her seat. "Morgan, right?" I nodded and returned her smile.

Mason let out a loud groan and looked at the sky with pleading eyes. "Please, please, can't you just get her laid so she can f*cking leave me alone?"

"Circle up, everyone! It's time for seven minutes in heaven!" Richard exclaimed as he shook a beer bottle in his hand. Mason stood up and followed the crowd while Lacey raised an eyebrow at me expectantly.

"I think I'm fine here," I told her with an awkward smile.

"Don't be ridiculous. It'll be fun!" she exclaimed and proceeded to drag me towards the circle. I desperately searched for Dee but failed to spot her. I cursed under my breath as I watched Richard set the bottle in the middle. There was a total of about twelve people sitting in the circle.

That was a pretty big number. What were the odds that I was going to get chosen? There was a loud cheer as soon as the first couple walked towards the closet. "So what? Do we just sit here for the next seven minutes?"

Lacey pursed her lips at my question then shrugged. "I've actually never played this game. I'm just trying to get with Mason, but he doesn't seem to be into me."

I winced. *Ah, I'm bad at dealing with emotional teenage girls.*

"Maybe he's just having a bad day," I said, hoping she would just nod and keep her problems to herself.

I wasn't so lucky.

Lacey shook her head. "I don't think it's that. I mean, I heard from a few girls that I shouldn't get my hopes up because all he mainly wants is sex, but he looks like he enjoys talking to me. What do you think?"

Quick, think of something girly to say.

I stared at her brown eyes with sorrow and bit my bottom lip nervously. "I think, ahh, I think you should just give it a shot to see if it works out."

"What if I get my heart broken?"

"Ah," I hummed awkwardly as I watched the couple exit the closet. *What if I just make a run for it? It's not like I talk to Lacey at school.*

"Your turn," Richard said, smirking. I silently thanked him for saving me from the most awkward conversation of my life.

I hesitantly twisted the bottle and painfully watched it land on . . .

Whatever your guess was, there was no way you're right. Richard looked at me in pure delight as he laughed out. "Aren't you the closet girl? What's your name, sweetheart?"

I ignored the first part as I stared at the bottle. I was wide-eyed with my jaw to my feet. "M-Morgan," I stammered.

"Morgan and Lacey!" he announced, earning a number of howls from a few guys. Lacey stood up and shook her head.

"No, I'm not playing."

Richard pouted and shook his head. "Sorry, babe. Once you're in the game, you can't back out."

"Don't be a dick, Venice," Mason called out from where he was sitting. Richard raised his brow and scoffed. "You want to lecture me on being a dick? Out of all people? Why don't you replace Lacey then, Hunter?" Richard shot back.

Everyone went silent as they watched Mason carefully. The reason Mason was a complete loner wasn't because no one liked him. It was because people feared him. Many guys idolized him for his success with the ladies but didn't dare talk to him.

Which is why everyone expected Mason to beat the living sh*t out of Richard. Mason smiled sarcastically and set his beer bottle down. "F*ckface, you coming?"

I looked at Richard pleadingly. "The only people I'd make out with is literally anyone else," I stated but only received an apologetic smile from Richard.

I swore as I shut the closet door. I couldn't really see anything, which calmed my nerves a bit. "I never really—ah," I yelped as I felt his hand brush my thigh.

"Don't worry, f*ckface. I wasn't planning on actually making out with you," he assured. My heart sped up as I felt his breath fan across my face, a sign that he was a little too close.

17

"M-Mason," I squeaked.

"What?"

"Can you back up a bit?"

"Or else what?" he challenged as he moved closer. His body was already flushed to mine, and if he moved any closer, our lips would be touching.

I put my hands on him in an attempt to push him back but stopped when I felt him stiffen.

"Mason?"

"Yeah?"

"Why is your phone in your tummy?"

"That's not my phone."

I was paralyzed and neither of us made a move to back off from each other. There was no way this was happening to me.

"Please tell me you have a rock in your pants, and if it isn't a rock, then please lie to me," I pleaded.

"Your hand is on my dick," he explained abruptly with a monotonous voice, almost as if he wasn't fazed by the situation.

I screamed and pushed him back. "Why did you get so close to me?" I could basically see Mason glaring at me.

"I was messing with you! You're the one who decided to go around and grab dicks. Don't blame this on me."

"Why was it—oh God, why was it so hard?" I stammered.

"I hate to break it to you, Morgan, but when girls go around touching my dick I—"

"Time's up!" Richard raised his eyebrows at us suggestively. "Wow, both of you look hella flushed. What were you guys doing?"

"I'd rather not talk about it." I shook my head.

CHAPTER FOUR
Don't Pity Him

MASON HUNTER

I smirked as I took a few steps forward.

"M-Mason," she stuttered.

"What?" I questioned. I hoped she couldn't see the malevolent smile on my face.

"Can you back up a bit?"

"Or else what?" I retorted and took a few steps further. I smirked proudly as I heard her breath hitch at our proximity. She put her hands on me to push me away, I suppose, and then I stiffened.

Why is she touching my dick?

"Mason?"

"Yeah?"

"Why is your phone in your tummy?"

I felt my pants tighten uncomfortably and shifted slightly, but I didn't move away from her. "That's not my phone," I murmured painfully.

There was an awkward silence. Neither of us were moving away.

She finally spoke, "Please tell me you have a rock in your pants, and if it's not a rock, then please lie to me."

Is she really that dense?

"Your hand is on my dick."

Morgan let out a yelp and pushed me back. I couldn't tell what she was doing, but she was moving around way too much. "Why did you get so close to me?" she exclaimed.

I glared at what I hoped was her face. "I was messing around! You're the one who decided to go around and grab dicks! Don't blame this on me."

"Why was it—oh God, why was it so hard?" she stuttered.

I licked my lips. I was glad it was dark, so she couldn't see the embarrassment on my face.

Say something, anything.

"I hate to break it to you, Morgan, but when girls go around touching my dick I—"

"Time's up!" Richard raised his eyebrows. "Wow, both of you look hella flushed. What were you guys doing?"

"I'd rather not talk about it."

I glared at Venice and clicked my tongue. "Don't worry about it."

I turned to look at Morgan, and as Venice had suggested, her face was as red as a tomato. Her eyes were darting around the room, looking at anyone but me.

"Damn, okay," Venice said as he raised his arms in surrender. "Let's choose the next pair then." I rolled my eyes before walking towards the door. I needed to smoke.

"I-I'm sorry," an irritating voice spoke as I finally reached Venice's backyard.

I lit the cigarette and watched as Pete pushed some other guy into the pool.

"For touching my dick? No problem." I shrugged as I took a drag of the cigarette. I needed a damn distraction. I didn't want to talk to her about how I had gotten a boner just by simply touching me.

She shushed me and looked around, her face turning red again. "Shut up."

20

After a couple of moments, she gazed at the cigarette. I looked at her in annoyance. "What?"

"Can I try it?" she asked with her eyebrows raised.

I had never really spoken to Morgan, but from what I heard about her, she wasn't the kind of girl to get mixed up with the wrong crowd, much less a girl who smoked. Yeah, she was a little weird and crazy, but she was the kind of girl who avoided guys like me at all cost.

But for some reason, she just wouldn't f*cking leave me alone. I never thought I would be running away from a girl.

"You want one?" I raised a brow. She didn't look like the kind of girl who smoked.

"Yeah," she responded.

"Then go buy some. I'm not going to be responsible for f*cking up your lungs."

She pursed her lips as she watched me step on the cigarette.

"Dick," she murmured under her breath and started to walk in the other direction.

*　　*　　*

The next morning, I woke up to screaming. It was like clockwork every Sunday morning. Every time I was woken up, I would always see Michelle sitting next to my bed in tears. "What's wrong, kiddo?" I asked groggily while she wiped her tears off her cheeks with the back of her hand.

My head was killing me, but I still managed to hold up a smile.

"Diane and Robert are fighting again," she whispered in a soft voice.

I sighed as I picked her up and seated her on my lap.

"How about we listen to some music?" I asked, hoping it would drown out their screams.

Michelle was another foster kid who had been wronged by the system. She was six years old stuck with foster parents who didn't give a dump and a foster brother who couldn't do sh*t about anything.

"I don't want to be here," she whimpered as she buried her face in my chest.

I stood up and kneeled next to her. "We can sneak out, but you need to be very quiet."

I doubt Diane and Robert would give a f*ck if I sneaked out. As long as they got their paycheck, they were fine, but they would care if Michelle would go missing. Losing a child wasn't a thing you wanted to explain to the agency.

Michelle nodded her head eagerly, making her black curls jump along with her.

"Let's do it then."

After I snuck Michelle out, I drove to the only place I knew. I knocked on the door hesitantly. "Whose house is this, Mason?" Michelle asked as she stared in awe at the house.

"A friend's."

A woman around the age of forty opened the door and gave us a questioning look.

"Is Morgan here?" I asked and gave her the best smile I could muster.

An emotion flashed past her eyes as she opened her mouth various times, almost as if looking for the right words to say. I couldn't blame her. I was probably the last kid she wanted her daughter to hang out with. I looked like trouble.

"Who are you?" she finally said.

"I'm Mason, ma'am, one of her friends," I stated. The words seemed foreign to me. "This is my sister, Michelle."

She smiled brightly and opened the door. "Morgan, you have visitors!"

Morgan popped out from a corner, looking like absolute hell.

Her brown hair was up in a messy bun. She was wearing sweatpants, and there was a bit of cheese dust on the corner of her mouth.

She looked like she had just woken up, and it was already 1 PM.

"Mason?" she said, confused. Her eyes then drifted towards Michelle.

"Hey, I was around the neighborhood and thought I'd pay you a visit."

Morgan furrowed her eyebrows but gestured to me to follow her.

"Keep the door open!" her mother exclaimed.

I held the urge to roll my eyes. *What can we possibly do with a kid sitting next to us?*

Since I was sober, this was the first time that I ever got to really look around her room. Her walls were pastel pink with posters of boy bands pasted everywhere. Her bed was decorated with pink pillows and stuffed animals. To complete everything, there was a large pile of clothes on a chair in the corner.

"I'm sorry for the mess. I wasn't expecting anyone," she murmured and scratched the back of her neck awkwardly.

"Wow," Michelle gasped from my side before I could say anything. "Can I play with your stuffed animals?"

Morgan's green eyes softened as she watched Michelle. "Yeah," she responded softly.

Michelle smiled and made a run towards the bed before hugging the stuffed animals tightly.

She hissed lowly and narrowed her eyes in suspicion. "What are you doing here, and while you're at it, you can explain how you know where I live."

"I used to go on your bus. Do you not remember?"

Yeah, then I was moved to a different foster family.

She nodded her head. "That still doesn't explain why you're here."

23

"My foster parents are fighting, and she doesn't want to be home. I don't know where else to take her."

Her eyes shone with sympathy as she frowned. Her lips parted before slamming shut again. I knew what she was going to say.

"Don't say anything. I don't want your pity. I just need to stay here for a while if that's okay."

"Yeah, that's fine."

CHAPTER FIVE
Stay in the Truck

MORGAN COLLINS

I glared at the time and tapped my foot anxiously. That slut was thirty minutes late.

"Out of all places you could have gone to."

I looked up and found Mason wearing an apron and looking annoyed as always. "What are you doing here?" I asked.

Mason looked at me as if I was stupid and gestured towards his uniform. "I work here," he answered dryly. I could feel my cheeks flare up as I looked down at my feet.

Oh.

"Well, you never know. What if that's just the way you like to dress?" I almost slapped myself at my response.

Morgan, you stupid piece of sh*t, why?

"Are you stoned?" he questioned. He was obviously cringing at my last comeback. I could hear the humor in his voice.

"I'm waiting for someone," I kept going, hoping he didn't see the embarrassment written all over my face.

"Your boyfriend?" he asked while the corners of his mouth turned up into a smirk. He knew I had no boyfriend.

I hissed at him. "This is why no one likes you." I expected him to roll his eyes and turn around, but he sat down and fiddled with the menu instead.

"You like me." He shrugged, almost as if he knew.

As if.

I rolled my eyes and slumped back in my seat, finally recovering from the embarrassment. "No, I don't."

His eyes shimmered with mischief as he leaned over and held my hands. "You don't?"

"N-no," I stuttered and drew my hands away quickly. "Stop being stupid."

"Then why are you so nervous?"

For starters, you are extremely close to me.

I narrowed my eyes. "You can't treat your customers like this."

He shrugged again and pulled back as if nothing had happened. "My shift is over."

My phone buzzed and I looked down.

Couldn't make it. Got grounded.

"Stupid Dee. She always does this," I hissed as I tossed my phone on the table. Mason raised a brow and an amused smile made its way onto his face.

"Got ditched?" he asked as he took a bite of the donut I had ordered.

"Yeah," I said and put my face in my hands. "She was my ride home." Mason raised his hands and his eyebrow.

"Calm down, f*ckface. There's no need to swear."

"Shut up," I growled. There was a short moment of silence before he stood up.

"I'll take you home," he said. I raised my head immediately.

"Really?" *Why is he being so nice to me?*

"Yeah." He tossed the keys towards me. "I'll pay for your donut. Just get in the car. It's a red truck. It's parked out front."

I took the keys and did as I was told, eventually finding his truck and starting it. "You're being nice," I said after we were both in the car. "Why?"

He raised an eyebrow at me and gave me a look. "You want me to be mean?"

"No!" I exclaimed abruptly, then brought my voice down after noticing how loud I had been. "I'm just asking."

Mason didn't take his eyes off the road. "You helped me out even though I've been nothing but rude to you. I thought I should return the favor."

A smile made its way onto my face as I scooted to the middle seat of his truck. "Does that mean we're friends?"

His smile dropped and he clenched his jaw. "Don't push it, f*ckface."

Okay, sheesh.

"You weren't supposed to turn here," I pointed out as I watched the street pass by.

"I know," he stated dryly. I opened my mouth to say something but debated against it. I shouldn't annoy him when he was finally starting to warm up on me. We suddenly stopped in front of a house, and he turned to look at me pointedly.

"Don't get off the truck and lock the doors."

I raised my brow but didn't question him. Mason jumped off and went inside the house. I made sure to lock the door like he said. The house looked old. The paint was chipped, and the grass was pretty much dead.

A knock on the window snapped me out of my train of thought. He was a middle aged man wearing a wifebeater stained with God knows what and jeans. He had his mail between his elbow and abdomen, a cigarette in his hand, and a scowl on his face.

I rolled down the window and smiled, but his face didn't budge. "You Mason's girl?" he spoke as he blew the smoke in my face.

Okay, rude.

"No, sir, just a friend," I clarified and held the urge to grimace at the smell. The man shook his head and flipped through his mail. "What's a girl like you doing with him?"

A girl like me?

"Robert," Mason spoke through his teeth. Robert threw him a disapproving look.

In a flash, Robert was in front of Mason with a hand in the air. "Don't you dare give me that tone, boy!"

From the corner of my eye, I saw Mason's foster sister flinch while Mason stood his ground. He rolled his eyes and snorted. "Why should I listen to a deadbeat like you?"

Robert brought his hand down and punched him. My eyes widened in horror as Mason fell and Robert climbed on top of him, throwing various punches.

"Mason!" Michelle exclaimed as tears streamed down her face.

"Get back in the house, Michelle!" Robert yelled before throwing his hands at Mason. "I'll show you who the f*ck you're talking to!"

I hesitated before running out of the truck just as a very thin woman exited the house.

"Robert, let go of him! The social worker is coming in a week!" she exclaimed and pulled Robert away from Mason. I expected to find Mason in tears or passed out, but he still had a smug smirk on his face.

"You're slacking, Rob. You haven't even made me pass out yet," he taunted, amusement lingering in his tone. I ran to Mason and helped him up with shaky hands, ignoring the look he gave me when I did.

Robert's face turned red at the comment, but he seemed to hold his temper this time. "I better not see you coming home tonight or I'll kill you."

"I'm taking Michelle," Mason stated, all traces of humor had left his tone as he started walking towards a very frightened Michelle.

Robert grabbed him from the back of his collar and pulled him back, sending Mason back to the ground. "You're not taking anyone," he spat.

"Listen, you f—" Mason started but was cut off by Robert's fist.

Mason laughed bitterly and spit out blood. "I've had worse." I went to stand in front of Mason as soon as Robert raised his fist again.

"Sir," I said, shaking with adrenaline. "If you hit him one more time, I swear I'll call the cops."

Robert lowered his fist, but the scowl was still etched on his face. "Get out of here, Mason, and take your little slut too."

Mason smiled softly and nodded at Michelle before standing up. "Let's go, Morgan." I gave Michelle a last look before climbing into the truck after him.

"I told you to stay in the truck," he said after a while. His lip was busted, his eyes were swollen, and he had cuts all over his face.

"Should you really be driving like that?" I asked with a raised brow.

Mason scowled and ignored my question. "Why did you get off the truck? What the f*ck would I do if he beat you too? You don't just jump in when a drunk is beating someone, Morgan," he scolded in a tone you would use when getting after a five-year-old.

"What was I supposed to do? Watch him punch you?" I exclaimed as I threw my arms in the air.

"You were supposed to mind your own business and stay in the truck."

My eyes widened in disbelief. "Why are you even dealing with him? You can just call the cops."

"Don't worry about it," he growled as he tightened the grip on the wheel. I sighed and slumped back in my seat, infuriated by the situation.

"You can stay at my house," I murmured softly. Mason didn't even turn to look at me as he stopped the truck in front of my house.

"No, thanks."

Fine. Screw you then.

I slammed his truck door shut and stormed into my house without saying another word.

CHAPTER SIX
Shower with Him

I woke up later that night by the sound of my window closing. "Oh no, you don't," I said and stood abruptly from my bed.

He had just told me he didn't need to stay at my place, and now he was here. Messy hair, tall, lean . . . He's so hot—no, Morgan, you're better than this!

"Please, Morgan, I have nowhere else," Mason said, his voice cracking a bit, making me halt. He was drunk, but he wasn't calling me any mean or confusing nicknames.

Mason's hair was in all directions, his shirt was wrinkled and backwards, and his belt was unbuckled.

His bruises had turned a sick purple color, but there were no traces of blood on his face.

"What happened?" I inquired, raising an eyebrow at his appearance.

Mason furrowed his eyebrows in disgust and shook his head. "Becky tried to have sex with me," he stated, sitting on my bed.

I sat next to him and scrunched my nose. He smelled like vomit and alcohol.

"I thought you are all about sex. Why did you pass on Becky?" I scooted a few inches away from him.

Becky was the captain of the wrestling team, and she was a goddess. She had an amazing curvy body, long brown hair, and big blue eyes. She looked like an angel even though she was anything but one.

Mason shook his head and gave me a lopsided smile. "You shouldn't judge a book by its cover." He scoffed.

I raised an eyebrow. "You told me you f*ck everyone, remember?"

He shook his head and looked down at his hands. "I was trying to be a dick. I've only ever been with one girl."

I turned my head so fast that I almost got whiplash.

"No way."

There was no way that Mason only ever had sex with one girl. All he reeked of were sex and sh*t at the moment.

"I swear," he continued, a smirk making its way to his face. "Besides you, I've never told anyone that I've f*cked. Most of the girls just make up the rumors. I just never bother to confront any of them."

My jaw fell open and I shook my head. *Impossible.*

He stretched his arm, and I almost fainted at the smell. "You need to shower, dipsh*t," I said and pinched my nose.

Mason sniffed his collar, making a face before nodding. "Yeah."

"The shower is at the end of the hallway to your right. I can get you some of my dad's clothes, but I can't promise any undergarments."

Mason shrugged and winked. "I'll fly solo."

Before he could say anything else, I tippy-toed my way to the laundry room. I was surprised to find my dad in the living room when I came out. He was usually asleep by nine.

My hands flew back, trying to hide his clothes from him. "What are you still doing, Dad? It's almost eleven."

"Your mom wanted to watch a movie. What do you have back there?" He shrugged and then raised an eyebrow at me.

I laughed nervously and started backing away. I had always been a terrible liar. "It's clothes, for me! You know, I'm going to shower! No further questions. Gotta go, bye."

I made sure to scram before he could ask another thing.

I opened the door to the restroom, sighed in relief once I heard the shower running, and locked the door behind me.

Mason peeked his head out of the shower and smirked. "If you wanted to join me, you could have just said so."

I snorted and sat on the toilet. "Don't be ridiculous. I'm just taking precautions."

"Whatever," he murmured accusingly and went back in the shower.

There was a sudden knock and my eyes widened.

"Honey, I forgot my phone on the counter! I'm gonna go in to get it!" my dad spoke.

F*ck, f*ck, f*ck!

"I'm not decent, Dad!" I screamed back and scowled at the black phone sitting on the counter.

"Just jump in the shower, honey. I'm just going to go in and out!"

Mason peeked out again and looked at me in panic.

I furrowed my eyebrows and shook my head before jumping in the shower with him. "Okay, Dad! Come in!"

I heard the door unlock and glared at Mason, trying to look at anywhere but his junk. The smirk on his face was huge.

Then the unbelievable happened.

I f*cking slipped and held on to Mason for support, only to have him fall on top of me.

I let out a yelp as I felt him land on top of me. Thankfully we were still in the shower, and he didn't make a sound.

"You okay?" I heard my dad ask.

"Yeah, I'm fine." My voice came out strained due to Mason still being on top of me.

"You sure you don't want me to call your mom?"

33

"No!" I blurted out. "I'm fine, I'm fine."

I heard the door close and glared at Mason, whose smirk doubled.

I hissed. "Get the f*ck off me."

He stood up and I regretted it immediately. His junk was right in front of my face.

"Don't f*cking say a word," I said. I felt the heat rush to my face.

I jumped out of the restroom, grabbed a towel, and stormed back into my room.

I took off the wet clothes and threw on another pair while trying to get the image of Mason out of my brain. I laid out a few blankets on the floor for him before jumping onto the bed. I forced my eyes shut.

Tomorrow would be another day.

*   *   *

"F*ck." I heard someone groan.

I almost jumped up in surprise when I felt an arm wrapping around my waist.

"Mason . . ." I trailed off slowly.

"What?" I could hear the pain and grogginess in his voice. He probably had a major hangover.

"What are you doing on my bed?"

His arm left my waist, and I could feel him rise. "I don't even remember coming to your house."

I shook my head and slumped back down. "Well, you need to leave."

I felt the bed shift. "Yeah, I know," he murmured. He still sounded half asleep.

"Thank you, Morgan," he said but I didn't answer.

I still hadn't gotten over the fact that I saw his . . . you know.

34

"You don't remember anything from last night, right?"

"Not a thing," he managed to say as I heard the window open.

"Good."

CHAPTER SEVEN
Hit Him Where It Hurts

Dee furrowed her eyebrows and plopped down on the bleachers. "Man, I didn't know it was this serious," she murmured as she watched teachers scurrying around with lists.

"Students, please refrain from leaving the gym or getting near the doors. We have just been informed that there is a tornado warning," a teacher spoke through a megaphone.

Dee pulled out her phone and sighed when she saw it had no signal. "Great," she murmured.

I held the urge to laugh at her behavior and shook my head. "This sucks," I murmured.

"Can I talk to you in private?"

Dee and I turned around to find Lacey standing next to us, wearing her blue and white cheerleading uniform.

"Yeah . . ." I trailed off and shrugged when Dee gave me a questioning look.

I followed Lacey to the corner of the gym and raised my eyebrows.

"You knew I liked him," she murmured accusingly as her eyes narrowed into small slits.

B*tch, what the f*ck?

"You mean Mason?" I inquired and stepped back when she poked me with her manicured finger.

Lacey hissed sarcastically. "No, the janitor. Yes, Mason! You went in the closet with him even though you knew I liked him!"

I was f*cking shocked. My eyes widened in disbelief at the once sweet girl who was now looking at me with pure hatred. It had been almost a week since that party. Why was she only confronting me about it now?

"Nothing happened," I clarified, raising my hands up in surrender.

You know, I just touched his dick, then showered with him. No biggie.

"Sure, nothing happened. I want you to stay away from him." She scoffed.

At the moment, that wouldn't be a big problem. I had been avoiding him ever since the . . . situation in my shower.

However, my stubborn ass wouldn't take it from her.

"You're like ninety pounds. What are you going to do? Beat me up?"

Lacey was a small red head. She was usually the girl on top of the pyramid since she was so light. I was way bigger than her for about twenty pounds. *There is no way she can beat me up, right?*

"Watch your back," Lacey said before turning on the balls of her feet.

Who was I kidding? She was going to cheer kick me into another dimension. I turned around and almost let out a scream when I bumped into Mason.

"Dude, I should give you a bell," I claimed as I put my hand in my chest in a sad attempt to slow down my heartbeat.

"You're avoiding me," he said.

"Hey, Morgan, how are you doing?" I mocked in the deepest voice I could muster, hoping he would crack a smile.

His expression didn't change. *Typical Mason.* "I thought you wanted me to leave you alone?" I stated and crossed my arms.

37

Who understood this guy? One day he wanted me to never talk to him again, and the next he wanted to be my friend. Whoever said that women were the complicated ones had never met Mason.

"That was before you took a good look at my balls and didn't call back the next day," he murmured, humor laced in his tone, but his expression stayed the same.

My face dropped and my eyes widened. "I thought you don't remember . . ."

There was a silence before Mason raised his eyebrows. "I was joking, f*ckface. Jeez, what the f*ck happened last night?"

Oh, crap.

"Nothing!" I said hurriedly and shook my head. "I was joking too!" I laughed nervously and scratched the back of my neck, hoping he would take the bait.

He didn't.

"You're a horrible liar," he suggested. His eyes suddenly widened, and the color drained from his face.

"We didn't . . . ?" He made a gesture between us.

"No, we didn't. Nothing happened," I lied and licked my lips. I remembered how he told me that he had only ever been with one girl.

"The corner of your mouth fidgets," he mentioned abruptly as if I would know what the f*ck he was going on about.

"What?"

"When you lie, you start nodding and the corner of your mouth fidgets. That's how I know you're lying."

*Observant f*ck. What do you even say to that?*

"So why don't you make it easier for the both of us and tell me the truth?" He gestured for me to continue.

I took in a deep breath and let everything out. "I'm, uh, avoiding you because I saw your dick in the—" I started to say rapidly.

"Wait, you what?"

"Students, stay away from the doors!" I heard a teacher exclaim.

Mason grunted as he flicked his wrist dismissively at the teacher. "F*ck off. What were you saying?"

"Excuse me?" the teacher shrieked in horror and started making her way towards us.

My eyes widened and my hands started to shake, not knowing what to do.

"Did I s—"

Before Mason could finish his sentence, the lights went out and screams filled the gym.

I took his hand and pulled him into the other direction, praying the teacher didn't see our face.

Mason grunted as he struggled to catch up with me. "Morgan, wait."

My foot got caught in something. I fell, tugging Mason along with me.

I turned my body upwards in hopes of saving my face from hitting the floor, only to have Mason land right on top of me.

Mason somehow managed to fly a bit farther than me though, which caused his crotch to land right on—you guessed it—my f*cking face.

Yeah, add that to the list of awkward things that had ever happened to me.

"Sh*t," Mason groaned in pain as he rolled off me.

I, on the other hand, just laid there.

*Someone up there must hate the living sh*t out of me.*

The lights turned on suddenly and everyone cheered, but I didn't dare move a muscle.

"Come on, get up," Mason murmured in a strained voice from my side while I watched him hold his crotch.

I stood up without saying a word and almost screamed out in desperation.

It couldn't be anything else. It had to be his dick landing right into my face. His dick had something against me. There was no other reason, no other explanation.

"Agree to never talk about this again?" he said as he limped, earning a few questioning glances from some students.

"Agreed."

CHAPTER EIGHT
Catch Him in the Act

"Collins!" Coach Sicowich exclaimed and blew his whistle aggressively.

I held the urge to roll my eyes at him. I smiled as best as I could while I made my way towards him. "Yes, Coach?"

Coach Sicowich was that forty-year-old bald, overweight, and bitchy P.E. coach in school. No one liked him, but no one wanted to get on his bad side either.

"Go get the dodgeballs from the storage room out back," Sicowich ordered as he handed me some keys.

Anything to get me out of running laps.

"And make sure you come back." He looked at me pointedly. Most kids just ditch after being sent out.

I took the keys from his hands and started walking towards the back of the gym.

Man, I f*cking hated P.E. There was nothing more that I detested than running laps. It was like having a sixty-year-old smoker's lungs. I could be three steps away before coughing up my organs.

I heard giggling and halted.

Oh no, this is the place where everyone makes out.

There was a blind spot for the cameras between the gym and the locker rooms.

I hastily passed the couple and walked a few more rooms until I finally reached the storage room.

"F*cking, Sicowich," I murmured and put the keys in the lock.

Huh, it is already unlocked.

"Mason," a moan came from inside the storage room, but my brain didn't have enough time to react. I flung the door open.

I saw Mason's dick for the second time this month.

"F*ck!" I exclaimed and shut the door.

Lacey and Mason were . . . in school? Why?

After remembering Coach's words, I hesitantly opened the door, making sure to look the other way.

"Can you pass me the dodgeballs?"

"No," Mason murmured.

There was shuffling before I felt a small hand on my shoulder, making me turn around.

"I'm sorry you had to see that," Lacey said, now fully clothed. Her cheeks were tinted with pink. I guess she had changed back into regular Lacey and not the evil cheerleader.

Sorry won't make me forget the atrocities I just witnessed.

"Yeah," I responded dryly and watched Lacey walk the other direction.

"What the hell, Mason?" I questioned. Fortunately, he was fully clothed now and was looking at me with a raised eyebrow. "Do you know what they could do to you if they found you were having . . . you know in school?"

Mason scoffed and adjusted his belt. He rolled his eyes while he reached for his jacket.

"That's none of your business," he murmured bitterly.

He tried passing me but I pushed him back into the closet, closing the door behind me.

"Mason, what's wrong with you?" I pushed and watched as his eyes shone with annoyance.

"I like to f*ck girls, Morgan. What do you want me to say?"

42

I winced at his response. He tried to get past me again, so I stepped sideways in order to block him.

"You told me you've only been with one girl," I stated.

Mason sighed and sat down on one of the shelves, finally realizing I wasn't going to let him out anytime soon.

"When did I tell you that?" he inquired, glaring at the wall behind me.

He looked like a child who had just gotten scolded for talking back.

"You were drunk," I clarified and put a hand on his shoulder. "Now tell me what's w—"

He snorted loudly then stood up abruptly as if my hand burned him. "Poor naive b*tch." He chuckled bitterly.

My mouth fell open and I gasped. "Excuse me?"

This f*cking b*tch wanted to fight me.

He crouched in front of me, so we were on eye level as his mouth contorted into a smirk.

"I lied," Mason admitted. The smirk never left his face.

"No, you didn't," I shot back stubbornly. There was no way he lied. There had to be a reason for his sudden mood swings. I mean, why would he pretend to be my friend if I annoyed him so much?

Unless . . .

"Were you just trying to get into my pants?" I asked as the sudden realization came to me.

Mason grimaced at the idea. "F*ck no," he said, almost growling. "You're awkward, annoying, and you look like you came out of a f*cking horror movie."

I frowned but didn't deny it. I mean, he wasn't wrong.

"So why make me believe we are finally friends if you're so annoyed with me?" I questioned, feeling my blood boil.

"I used you," he replied, his smirk growing bigger. "I needed a place to stay. It's not rocket science, Morgan."

I clenched my fist and narrowed my eyes, building up the courage for what I was about to do.

"Now, go run along. Also, just f*cking leave me alone for once in your—"

I threw my hands up and punched him square in the jaw, cutting him off abruptly. I knew he didn't need any more people hitting him, but he had my blood boiling at this point. He shouldn't have taught me how to punch.

I really need some anger management classes.

"I f*cking sw—"

I went to throw another punch, but he caught it quickly.

He tightened his grip on my fist and I winced.

"Your mistake was believing in me," he grunted before releasing my fist. I watched him storm out of the closet.

*   *   *

"What's wrong with you two?" Dee raised her eyebrow and nudged my side later that week.

It's been a week since our encounter in the storage room, and I had been avoiding Mason up until now.

"Nothing," I stated as I tossed a french fry into my mouth.

Dee gave me a pointed look and gestured towards Mason with her spork. "I would believe that a little more if you stopped shooting glares at him every ten seconds."

He had been avoiding me too. In anatomy, he sat with Patricia Edwards. Now he was sitting with the cheer squad.

"He's being a dick." I shot yet another glare towards him.

"Mason? Being a dick? No!" Dee exclaimed in a monotonous voice. "Do you know why no one ever talks to Mason, Morgan?"

"Because he's a dick," I repeated as I fiddled with the limp tomato on my plate.

"Because he doesn't want any friends. Do you think you're the first person to ever try to become his friend? He pushes them all away, or he f*cks and then ditches them," Dee retorted as she threw a look at the cheer squad.

I shook my head and looked back down at my feet.

"I just can't believe he lied."

Dee gave me a look. "He has a reputation for it, honey. How did you not see it coming?"

She has a point.

"Okay. From now on, I'm not going to mess with boys who have a stick shoved up their ass."

"Amen," Dee replied.

CHAPTER NINE
Get a Little Help from a Jock

Richard Venice sat next to me in anatomy and smiled when I raised a brow at him.

"Can I help you?" I asked, a bit shocked by the whole situation.

Richard was the typical popular jock who hosted all the rocking parties, but he wasn't that mean cliché character you heard about in every movie either.

For a football player, he was a bit thin, but that didn't keep him away from being attractive with his long blond hair and warm greenish eyes.

"Your boyfriend took my partner." He gestured at the back of the room where Mason was sitting with one of the pretty volleyball players.

"He's not my boyfriend," I murmured and looked back at the front of the class. Mrs. Porter was babbling about her life as she usually did.

Richard gave me a look as if telling me he knew what I meant. "Trouble in paradise," he confirmed and nodded his head slowly.

"No. We were never together," I growled.

"Okay, sure. Whatever, Morgan." Richard shrugged sarcastically and paid attention to the teacher.

After a while, Richard decided to let out another painful stream of words as if I wasn't annoyed enough.

Now I knew how Mason felt whenever I tried talking to him.

"I can help you get him back," he said.

I rolled my eyes but didn't turn to look at him. "I don't want him back. Plus, we were never dating," I repeated. *Can't this guy take the hint?*

Richard shrugged and clicked his pen. "I don't know. I've never seen him talk more to a girl than you."

I scoffed and held the urge to point out all the girls he'd been with so far.

It's funny how he had never been seen with so many girls, then he would tell me how he wasn't really a wh*re. Then suddenly, he started banging anything with legs.

"Sure," I let out sarcastically.

"You know what, Morgan? I'm going to help you."

"Literally, no one is asking for your help," I said, putting my head in my hands.

"No, I insist."

Great.

*   *   *

MASON HUNTER

I sat down and buried my head in my hands, not giving a sh*t if I was missing calculus.

I knew I should be happy that Michelle was finally going to get adopted, that she was finally getting an out, but I wasn't. I was furious.

I wanted to keep her with me. I knew it was selfish, but she was the closest thing to a family that I had. I didn't want to let her go.

"F*ck," I growled as I pulled on my hair.

The universe really loved to screw with me.

"What's wrong?"

I looked up and saw Lacey wearing the school uniform even though her skirt was hitched a bit higher than the school would've liked.

I scowled. "Please leave me alone, Lacey." I put my head back down, hoping she'd take the memo and walk away.

I wasn't in the mood to talk to anyone. I didn't give a f*ck who it was.

Lacey set a hand on my shoulder as her eyes flashed with sympathy.

"I can help you not think about it," she smiled as she leaned over a bit to show her cleavage through the school's button-up shirt.

Lacey really didn't seem like the girl to give herself out like this. Maybe she wanted to prove people that she was different from what everyone else thought or maybe she was just bored.

Whatever it was, I didn't give a flying f*ck. If this had been any other day, I would've rejected her offer, but I really needed a distraction.

I nodded and she stood up quickly, pointing towards the gym.

"I know the perfect place."

And that was how I found myself in a closet arguing with Morgan.

"What the f*ck, Mason?" Morgan was standing in front of the storage room, looking at me as if I had gone crazy. "Do you know what they could do to you if they found you were having . . . you know in school?"

I scoffed and buckled my belt, rolling my eyes while I reached for my jacket.

I wasn't in the mood to argue with her either.

"That's none of your business," I murmured bitterly.

48

I tried passing her, but she pushed me back into the closet roughly and closed the door behind her.

I could feel anger starting to build at the pit of my stomach. What the f*ck was she doing here messing with me? She could have been anywhere, but here she was, f*cking with me when I was no good for her.

"Mason, what's wrong with you?" she said again.

I held the urge to roll my eyes. She was acting as if she knew me.

"I like to f*ck girls, Morgan. What do you want me to say?"

I made another move to pass her, but she stepped to the side, successfully blocking me.

"You told me you've only been with one girl," she stated as a matter of fact.

*When the f*ck did I tell her that?*

I sat down on one of the shelves after sighing. Morgan wasn't going to let me leave, I was sure of that.

"When did I tell you that?" I voiced my thoughts, glaring at the wall behind her.

"You were drunk." She put a hand on my shoulder. I felt another rush of anger surge through my body. Did she not get that I didn't want to be friends with her? She should be hanging out with other people, better people.

"Now tell me what's w—"

"Poor naive b*tch," I snorted loudly, then stood up abruptly.

In her defense, she was cute and maybe a little funny. However, I needed to get rid of her or I would either drag her down with me or she would annoy me to the point where I would find the need to strangle her.

Maybe we could've been friends in another life.

"Excuse me?" she gasped. Her face flushed and her green eyes widened dramatically.

I crouched down, not forgetting to flash her my signature smirk.

"I lied," I murmured.

I didn't. I had only been with one other girl. Well, two now if you count Lacey, but why did it matter now?

"No, you didn't," she shot back stubbornly.

I almost let out a groan of desperation. Did I have to scream it at her? Why wouldn't she get the memo?

"Were you just trying to get into my pants?"

I tried my best to look disgusted, but in all honesty, she wasn't that bad. Maybe if she didn't talk as much.

"F*ck no. You're awkward, annoying, and you look like you came out of a f*cking horror movie," I hissed.

"So why make me believe we were finally friends if you're so annoyed with me?" she questioned. I could tell she was getting angry by the way she clenched her fist.

"I used you. I needed a place to stay. It's not rocket science, Morgan," I answered.

She's been nothing but nice to you, my conscience reminded me and I cursed it.

It wasn't her fault I was so f*cked up. She didn't deserve this, but I wasn't going to drag her down with me. I also wasn't going to let her deal with all the sh*t in my life.

Finish it, Mason. You're doing the right thing.

"Now, go run along. Also, just f*cking leave me alone for once in your—"

I suddenly felt a sharp pain in my jaw and tried to not look so surprised.

She has one hell of a right hook.

"I f*cking sw—" I started but was distracted by her fist flying my way.

I caught her fist before it could reach me and put a bit of pressure, hoping it wouldn't hurt too much.

50

I had my fair share of fights. The only person I wasn't willing to hit was Rob. Mostly because it would be hard to explain why both him and his foster kid had bruises. Also Morgan, because she was so small. I would probably break her in a second.

She gave a mean punch though.

"Your mistake was believing in me," I murmured truthfully before storming out of the closet.

I made sure to ignore the small ounce of regret tugging at my gut.

CHAPTER TEN
Throw Up on His Shoes

MORGAN COLLINS

"How is this supposed to help me?" I looked doubtfully at the cup Richard was offering me and took it. I had given up on rejecting Richard's offer to "help" since he wouldn't accept the fact that I didn't need any.

"It'll let you relax." He shrugged and nodded encouragingly.

I came to one of his parties when he claimed he had an idea. I just wanted him to f*cking leave me alone.

"I don't know. Every time a girl gets drunk in a book, she ends up getting raped," I said, realizing how idiotic I sounded once he raised his blond brow.

"Yeah, I have no idea what you're talking about," he said after a long silence.

I let out an airy sigh and examined the red solo cup once again.

Why did everyone buy these cups for a party? Was it like a party rule? What if you bought blue solo cups? Was your party not cool anymore?

"Here goes nothing," I mumbled and poured the liquid in my mouth. I hissed when it made its way down my throat.

Richard smiled and led me past the massive crowd.

"So what do you like to do, Morgan?"

I hummed and looked oddly at the cup. Huh, most girls in movies got drunk after literally one cup. Maybe I was doing it wrong.

"I like to watch Netflix a lot." I shrugged.

There was really nothing interesting about me. I really didn't do much. I just invested myself into school most of the time.

And mean, bad boys apparently.

"What is this?" I made a face as he handed me another cup. I hesitantly chugged it down. My head was starting to feel a bit fuzzy but nothing too serious.

"Vodka and cranberry juice," Richard said as we finally arrived in the backyard. He gestured to me to sit down with him on the hammock and passed me the last cup he had been holding.

"And why do I need to get drunk?"

Is he going to rape me? Oh no, does this have drugs in it?

"I don't know Mason that well. He comes to all my parties but that's it. Although I'm guessing that if he sees that I'm getting you drunk, he'll do something about it," he explained as he slowly started rocking the hammock.

Why am I listening to him again?

"Are you just going to stare at it all day?" He furrowed his brow. Oh yeah, he wouldn't leave me alone.

I chugged the drink down and groaned as I was starting to feel lightheaded.

"That should do it," he said and laid back on the hammock.

I followed the action and shivered. "Why didn't I bring a sweater?" I mumbled.

I felt the hammock shift, and before I knew it, Richard had draped his sweater on me.

"So, Morgan, what's up with you and Mason?" he finally said after a while. He turned his body towards me.

53

"Literally nothing." I snorted. I felt like I was here, but I wasn't. I felt weird. Everything was starting to become a big fuzz.

"So why are you making me do this then?" He chuckled and shook his head.

I gasped and turned my body towards him too. Our faces were inches apart at this point.

I shrieked. "I didn't make you do anything! You're the one who suggested we should do this even though I told you I had nothing to do with Mason!"

Richard hummed and stared at me with something unknown in his eyes. "Maybe I'm just doing it because I find you cute."

My heart sped up and I wondered if I heard that correctly. "Richard, w-what?"

Richard smiled and tucked a fraction of my frizzy brown hair behind my ear.

"Stop calling me Richard."

I frowned at this and pulled his hand back. "Isn't that your name?"

He chuckled and shifted a bit closer to me but made no move to touch me. "Yeah, but no one has called me that since third grade. I prefer you call me Venice."

There was a short silence, and I looked into his hazel eyes.

Is this just me being out of it? What the f*ck is happening?

He leaned over a bit, and I felt my heart stop. *Am I going to get my first kiss? Am I going to suck his dick? Ew. Was I going to suck his dick?*

Richard suddenly pulled back and shook his head.

"You're drunk, Morgan."

"Good. I didn't want to suck your dick."

He burst out laughing and shook his head, wiping a tear that had started to run down his cheek. "You weren't going t—"

"What the f*ck, Venice?" I heard Mason growl, and we both sprang up from the hammock.

54

"M-Mason?" I slurred.

"She's drunk? She's underage for f*ck's sake," Mason said.

Richard raised a brow. "So are you and me, and we drink all the time."

Mason towered over Richard easily.

"Yeah!" I agreed as I flung my arm around Richard. "And Richy is my friend!"

"Really? Because from the looks of it, he was about to take you on the hammock," he hissed. He shoved Richard back.

"Why do you care anyways? You don't even want to be my friend!" I exclaimed, not really caring that a crowd had started to form.

Mason's eyes darted back and forth. I assumed he felt uncomfortable with the sudden attention. He leaned a bit.

"I was angry. I told you that because I wanted you to stay out of trouble, but here you are with this f*ck! If I had known this was going to happen, I wouldn't have told you sh*t."

I crossed my arms and glared at him. "What—" I was cut off when I felt a large ball at my throat.

Oh, I didn't think that cranberry juice sat well with my stomach.

I lurched all the contents of my stomach onto Mason's shoes, and I heard him sigh.

"I'm taking her home." I heard him say.

Did I really just throw up in front of all these people? How embarrassing.

Mason pulled me towards him and sighed.

"You're a pain in my ass."

"I never asked you to help me, dickhole," I mumbled.

We started walking towards the parking lot. I halted once I saw his truck.

"Aren't you drunk too?"

He kicked off his shoes next to the trash can and took the keys from his jeans. "Nah, I didn't really drink."

I hummed in acknowledgement and kept walking. "I can't go home. I told my parents I would be sleeping at Dee's," I admitted bashfully as I climbed on his truck.

"Tough sh*t, that's what you get for getting drunk" he mumbled.

"Please," I pleaded and gave him the best puppy eyes I could muster.

"Do you want me to drop you off at Dee's then?" he said again and started the engine.

"I can't go to hers either, silly. She told her mom she would be sleeping at mine, but she actually w-went to see her ex-boyfriend." I giggled.

What am I laughing at again?

"Where were you going to f*cking sleep?" he asked and looked at me as if I was dumb.

"I w-was going to sneak back into my place at around four. I didn't know I'd leave t-this early." I giggled at the expression he had on his face. His eyebrows were furrowed, and his eyes were narrowed in disbelief.

"That sounds f*cking stupid."

The car ride to his house was very quiet. He didn't say anything until we were in his room.

"If you make a sound, we're both dead," he whispered as he gestured to me to take his bed. I nodded and started to unbuckle my jeans.

"W-what are you doing?" he asked, turning towards the other direction when I started pulling my jeans down.

"I can't sleep in jeans, silly. It's hot. It's not like you haven't seen any of this before."

"I'll get you some shorts," he said and walked into the restroom.

I laid down and covered myself in his sheets, inhaling deeply.

Was it weird that I liked how he smelled?

Morgan, you f*cking weirdo.

Ha, I called myself a weirdo.

When Mason came back, he had fully changed into shorts. He tossed me a plain shirt of his and some shorts.

I stared at his bare chest and almost drooled. He was so—

"You can change in the restroom. There's also an extra toothbrush in there. Make sure to tell me which one you used, so I can burn it after," Mason said in all seriousness and jumped in the bed.

"Mason," I mumbled to which he responded with a hum. "Where am I going to sleep?"

"The bed," he stated.

"But you're on it."

"If you want to take the floor, then there it is. I'm not giving up my bed just because you are stupid enough to get drunk."

I groaned and made my way towards the restroom.

Stupid boy.

CHAPTER ELEVEN
Help Him Find His Biological Parents

I cracked my eyes open and groaned when I realized it was already morning.

*What the f*ck is on my face, and why do I feel so heavy?*

My hand flew up to my face, and I groaned in disgust.

Ew, drool. Wait . . . I don't drool.

"Mason," I shrieked, finally realizing what was happening.

We somehow managed to tangle our legs and our bodies were pressed together. His arms were lazily wrapped around my body. To my dismay, a pool of his drool had started to form on my cheek.

Mason hummed but didn't open his eyes.

"Let go of me," I snarled and tried to pry myself away from him."

"Piss off," he groaned and pulled me even closer.

Huh, the bad boy likes to cuddle. Who would have known?

"I will rip your dick off if you don't let me go."

I heard him snoring lightly. I rolled my eyes.

"F*cking piece of sh*t, boy—" I froze as I felt something poke my thigh once I started to shift around.

"Oh, f*ck no, this is not happening again. M-MASON!"

"What?" he questioned. His face turned into an ugly scowl, but his eyes were still shut.

"W-what is that?" I stammered and made no move. I seriously had some ugly experiences with his dick.

"Calm down. It has nothing to do with you. It's just my morning wood," he murmured and finally let me go, turning his body away from me.

"Someone's knocking," I mumbled suddenly as I heard a series of knocks coming from the door.

"Mason, someone's knocking," I repeated when he didn't answer.

"Go open it then," he replied grumpily and rolled over again, shielding his face from the sun with his arm.

"I can't. Your foster parents might see me," I explained, hoping he would just get up and open the door.

No such luck.

"They're at work, so go open the door and leave me alone," he groaned.

"Michelle might see me then."

There was a short pause and a sigh from Mason. "She's not here either."

I made a sound in between a groan and a shriek and stood up angrily, not bothering to poke him on the subject. I had never been much of a morning person; apparently, neither was Mason.

I stormed my way to the door and opened it. There was a man on the other side. He looked around forty. His head was balding, and his glasses were too big for his face.

He smiled and looked at the paper he had on his hand. "I'm looking for Mason Hunter," he said and handed me a picture.

Staring back at me was a little boy with the same golden eyes Mason had, except the boy in the picture looked a lot happier than Mason.

"Yeah, can you hold on for a bit?" I mumbled groggily and walked back to Mason's room.

He had fallen asleep again.

"Mason, some guy is looking for you," I said, shaking him a bit.

Mason opened his eyes and glared but stood up nonetheless. I could hear him mumbling profanities under his breath.

"If you woke me up for nothing, I swear, Morgan," he growled and made his way towards the front door.

"Mason Hunter?" the man spoke, his eyes shining with hope.

"That's me," Mason said as he leaned over the door frame. "What can I do for you?"

The man cleared his throat and nodded, fumbling with the paperwork in his hand. "I am Nolan Matthews, a private investigator from Woodrow Falls. I have reason to suspect that you are Olivia and Ronald Warren's lost child, Alessandro Warren."

Mason's face didn't move a muscle, then he shook his head. "My biological parents gave me up. You have the wrong guy."

Before Mason could shut the door, Nolan spoke up, almost exasperated. "Alessandro has a birthmark on his chest, the one you bear," Nolan exclaimed as he handed Mason yet another picture of a baby with the same birthmark Mason had.

Whoa, this is getting intense.

"You need to come with me right away."

And so we did.

Apparently there was no time to drop me off, seeing that Woodrow Falls was four hours away.

I texted my parents a half-assed excuse, then put my phone away. I occasionally glanced at Mason, who was just glaring at the road for the whole ride.

Typical.

"Are you going to tell me what happened?" Mason questioned a bit rudely, but Nolan didn't seem to mind.

"You were kidnapped at age four in Woodrow Falls. Your parents hired me shortly after the police gave up. I spent months looking for you. Your family and I had lost hope and stopped the search until I saw those very familiar golden eyes at that diner a few weeks back," Nolan explained.

Um what?

"I did a lot more digging and found that the people who kidnapped you were arrested for human trafficking. They took all of you to foster homes as they couldn't find who you belonged to"

My eyes swung towards Mason, expecting him to look confused or even surprised, but he was wearing the cold nonchalant expression he always wore.

"Are you okay?" I wondered, noticing Nolan completely stopped the car.

"Peachy," he said through gritted teeth.

"We're here," Nolan said as he gestured to the house in front of us.

It was f*cking huge.

"Can I have time alone with my friend?" Mason scowled and Nolan nodded, leaving the vehicle.

I opened my mouth, finding the correct words to say, but came empty.

His fist were tightened and he was staring at the house hatefully.

The silence was killing me.

"While I was getting beat by different foster parents and getting starved, these f*ckers were over here living like this," Mason scoffed and gestured at the obviously luxurious house.

"Mason," I spoke softly and cupped his hand. Surprisingly, he didn't move back. "They tried looking for you."

Mason rolled his eyes. "Yeah, for a few months, then they just gave up on their missing kid."

I sighed. *What do you even say in a situation like this?*

"Give them a chance, Mason. They're your parents."

61

Mason said nothing as he swung the door open.

"Alessandro!" a woman exclaimed while running over to Mason, embracing him in a tight hug. The woman was incredibly small and shared no similarities to Mason. She was blonde, thin, and had piercing blue eyes.

A man emerged from the woman's side and also hugged Mason, but Mason just stood there limply. The man, on the other hand, was a copy of Mason. Both shared the golden eyes, the brown hair, and the strong nose.

The woman pulled back with tears in her eyes, finally noting me. "And who are you?"

"A friend," Mason spoke before I could answer, taking a few steps back. "And my name's Mason, not Alessandro."

I fumbled nervously on the side and shifted my gaze to literally anything else.

This is so f*cking awkward. F*ck.

"I don't care what you want to be called. I'm just so happy you're ba—"

"I'm not staying," Mason cut her off quickly and shook his head.

Olivia's face fell and Ronald furrowed his eyebrows.

"But we're your parents," Ronald said. The tone he had said it in had my heart breaking.

"You stopped looking and I was left to live a f*cking childhood with a bunch of people who couldn't give two sh*ts about me," Mason growled and shook his head.

I knew it wasn't my place but I stepped in, holding onto Mason's arm. "I think we should let him cool down and go back home before talking about coming to live with you guys."

Mason could say some pretty stupid sh*t when he was angry, but I knew anything was better than living with his foster parents.

Olivia nodded and rubbed the tears that had started to roll down her cheeks. "That'll give us some time to talk to the social worker."

Ronald started dialing a number. "I'll call a cab."

This sh*t was so f*cked up.

CHAPTER TWELVE
Finally Become His Friend

Richard set his tray down next to Dee. He smiled brightly when Dee gave him an odd look, then turned to me. "So, you and Mason are talking again?" Richard asked.

"Why is he sitting with us?" Dee gestured towards the jock, completely ignoring him.

Richard took a bite out of his fries and grinned, apparently not offended by Dee's question. "Hello to you too," he chuckled.

I hadn't filled her in with anything that happened last Friday, but to be fair, she hadn't filled me in with what happened with her ex-boyfriend, Troy.

"I don't want any of Troy's friends sitting on our table," she snarled.

It was safe to assume it didn't go well with her ex.

I looked at Richard, half expecting him to get up and walk away, but he threw her a smile instead. "Troy isn't my friend, sweetheart. I don't like the way he treats women."

Dee's brown eyes widened, then her jaw fell. "Wow, are you single?"

I almost choked on my fries as Mason sat down on my left side.

*Where the f*ck are they all coming from?*

So now Mason and I were facing Dee and Richard.

"Yes, I am but I kind of have my eyes on someone else."
Richard flicked his hazel eyes towards mine and winked.

This couldn't be happening. I felt eyes burning at the back
of my neck and almost sighed. I could hear the hushed whispers.

"Venice and Mason are sitting with the girl who threw up."

"Mason always sits alone though."

"She looks like a rat on—"

I glared at the last one even though she wasn't wrong. Man,
they really needed to learn how to whisper.

"I thought I told you Venice was no good," Mason
whispered, scowling at me.

*What is he mad at me for? I don't own the f*cking table!*

"I can still hear you even though you're whispering," he
suggested as he offered Mason an amused smile.

"I'm trying to be polite," Mason said in a deadpan manner
and started fiddling with the food on his plate.

I sighed and slumped down, sticking a fry in my mouth.
"Everything's fine," I murmured.

Richard shrugged. "Thanks for the effort."

"And I thought I had told you to get away from her,"
Mason mentioned, narrowing his eyes. If looks could kill, Richard
would be six feet underground.

"We're only having lunch, Hunter. I'm not finger banging
her under the table." Richard smiled smugly as he watched my face
go red. Why the f*ck was this happening to me? What did I do to
deserve this?

Dee sent me a look from across the table and raised her
eyebrows. "Lucky wh*re," she mouthed.

I'd switch places with her any day.

"Whatever," Mason murmured as he poked at his lunch.

"Well—" Dee said, suddenly standing up while sending me
an encouraging look "—I have things to do. Call me later,
Morgan."

I glared at her, fully aware of what she was doing. Mason and Richard murmured their "byes" but didn't give Dee another glance.

"F*ck you," I mouthed to which she responded with a wink.

"Why do you even care so much? Last week you were ignoring her," Richard questioned as a mischievous smile made its way onto his face.

I raised an eyebrow at this and awaited Mason's answer. Richard had a point.

"Because she's my friend," Mason muttered under his breath. I barely heard it, but he had said it.

"Ah, you finally admit that we're friends!" I cheered and slapped his arm playfully but only received a death glare in return.

Richard frowned mockingly. "Why can't I be your friend?" He pouted at Mason and wiped a fake tear for effect.

"Because I choose my friends depending on how much of a pain in my ass they are. Unfortunately, you're up there in the scale," Mason grumbled.

"Aw, I'm not a pain in your ass," I cooed and smiled at him.

He is starting to warm up on me.

"Oh no. You are a pain in my ass, but you have my back when I need you."

I frowned. *Maybe not.*

"So now that the best friend position is filled up, can I take the boyfriend position?" Richard brought up, earning a scowl from Mason.

I opened my mouth and closed it a few times, unsure of how to reply to that.

"Why don't you try to get in someone else's pants, Venice?" Mason glowered.

Richard rolled his eyes and stood up abruptly. "I'm playing, Hunter. No need to get your panties in a twist. I'll leave your best friend alone, or won't I?" He added a wink before suddenly taking off. "I'll leave you to being friendzoned. I have to go."

"What a tool." Mason shook his head as he watched him leave.

"He's nice," I defended and picked another fry, pouting at how soggy the ketchup had made it.

"He wants to get in your pants. He always wants my leftovers." He shook his head and rolled his eyes.

I furrowed my eyebrows at him. "I am not your leftover," I emphasized.

"I don't mean you, dumbass," he rolled his eyes.

"Then who do you mean if you've only been with a few girls?" I made finger quotations around the word 'few', referring to the past month.

Mason licked his lips hesitantly as if debating whether to tell me or not.

"I didn't lie about only being with one girl. Granted, I f*cked Lacey, but she was the only one that I f*cked after three years."

"What about the other girls?"

"I was messing with them. I wasn't going to have sex with some random girl. Do you think I want AIDS." He looked at me with a raised brow.

"Then what did you mean about Richard always wanting your leftovers?"

Mason sighed. "You weren't here freshman year, were you?"

I shook my head slowly. I had only gotten here at junior year, from hot and sunny Texas to gloomy Alaska.

"Believe it or not, I had a girlfriend during freshman year. Her name was Jessica. We made it through the year and eventually towards sophomore year too. I thought I loved her—" he took a deep breath "—we had a falling out and she went to one of

Venice's stupid parties. Of course, he couldn't keep his dick in his pants and made a move on her."

Oh no, that didn't sound good.

"He took her to the lake in back of his house, and while he left to get some f*cking blankets, she stepped on the ice. The ice was too thin, so she plummeted down and couldn't find her way out," Mason shrugged as if it was the most casual story he was telling.

I opened my mouth a few times but no sound came out. I didn't know what to say.

He continued, "Turned out, she had been cheating on me with Venice for months."

No wonder he has so much trouble opening up to girls.

"I'm sorry," I apologized.

"What did I tell you about pitying me, Morgan?" He raised an eyebrow.

"Sorry."

Mason rolled his eyes but threw an arm around me.

"Just try to avoid Venice, f*ckface."

CHAPTER THIRTEEN
Kiss Him

MASON HUNTER

"I swear," I grumbled angrily as I tried to muffle the sounds out with my pillow.

Robert and Diana were going at it again.

I turned and looked at the clock, almost wincing when I saw the time.

I didn't even have work until five in the afternoon.

"He's leaving. Now that we don't have Michelle, who are they going to give us a check for?" Diana exclaimed hysterically. She sounded close, like she was outside my door.

"What do you mean he's leaving?" Robert growled. The doorknob started to jiggle, and I held the urge to slam my head into the pillow.

I really need a f*cking vacation.

"The social worker says there are some people who want to adopt him. It'll take some time, so we'll still have checks rollin' in." She snorted.

Robert pulled me up from the collar and scowled. "You ain't going nowhere, you hear me, boy?"

"Don't you people have any respect?" I hissed groggily. I was just hoping he would let me sleep.

"You're not leaving," Robert snarled.

"Yeah, I'm not deaf. I heard you the first time," I shot back.

His ears turned bright red, and he raised his fist up in the air.

Robert always had trouble controlling his anger. I couldn't blame him. I liked to poke his buttons. He did make me wonder if his mother had poured drugs in his bottle before or after she dropped him on his head.

I smirked up at him. "Watch it there, Robert. Now that Michelle's not here, nothing's stopping me from running to the social worker or whooping your ass. Truthfully, it all depends on my mood."

Robert scoffed and pushed me back down. "Get the f*ck out of here."

That was basically how I found myself knocking on Morgan's window at nine in the morning on a Saturday.

She opened her window and rubbed her eyes, almost as if she couldn't believe that I was here.

Her hair was all over the place, and she was wearing an oversized shirt that stopped at her mid thigh.

I tried to keep my eyes above the hem of her shirt as I felt my jeans tighten slightly. Maybe I should go sleep in a dumpster.

"Can I help you with something?" She raised an eyebrow and squinted her eyes.

I shrugged but pushed myself in, nevertheless. I doubted her parents were even here due to the lack of cars in the driveway. "I was bored," I lied and sat on her desk.

I watched her sigh but drag herself back into bed. I didn't think she had noticed the fact that she was wearing no pants but my dick had.

I was tempted to let her know but finally debated against it.

"Okay, just be quiet," Morgan murmured as she pulled the covers on her.

"You can't go back to sleep," I stated and pulled the covers off her mockingly, trying to shift my eyes from her legs again.

"What the f*ck is your motherf*cking problem?" she growled and sat up when I had pried the covers away from her.

*F*ck, she is not a morning person.*

"What are you really doing here, sh*t for brains?" she hissed groggily.

"I needed to get out of the house," I shrugged, sitting down next to her. I made sure to wipe any traces of humor off my face.

She made a face before crossing her arms, apparently annoyed by what I had said. "I don't know why you're still taking their crap. Your real parents showed up."

I rolled my eyes.

"You're a rich girl who grew up with two loving parents and got everything you wanted. You wouldn't get it."

Morgan froze before clenching her fist. "It's not that hard, Mason. You'd be way better with your actual parents."

I tried to keep my cool, but this girl really knew how to push my damn buttons.

"F*ck off, Morgan," I said. I didn't need her to understand why I didn't want to go with my real parents.

I grew up alone because they had stopped looking. Morgan had and always would have everything. I didn't need her telling me sh*t out of all people. She poked my chest with her small finger and narrowed her eyes. "Don't tell me to f*ck off. You're in my house."

"Well, I wouldn't be in your house if you had just left me the f*ck alone!" I snarled and pushed her arm off my chest.

"You're the one who came into my room drunk and vulnerable!" She scoffed, her eyes widened in anger and she shoved me again.

"You could've sent me out. I didn't force you to help me!"

"You were bleeding," she emphasized. "Maybe if you hadn't been such a sh*t for brains, we would have never been in this mess!"

She reached to push me one more time, but I caught her arm just in time. I shoved her back and she fell onto the bed with a small "oof".

"Dumbass!" she growled and kicked me lightly.

I narrowed my eyes and climbed onto her, pinning both of her hands beside her head. "Again, I didn't force you to help me."

"So you remember!" she exclaimed as she trashed under me.

Of course I do.

Morgan growled in frustration at my silence. I didn't know if it was something in the air or how pissed we were or, to be honest, the fact that she wasn't wearing any pants. However, I couldn't help but notice our proximity.

I gulped as my eyes trailed down her body, noticing how her shirt had rode up onto her belly button, exposing her thighs fully.

I closed my eyes and blew out a shaky breath.

*Not her, Mason. Not—oh, f*ck it.*

Our lips met and she froze before returning the kiss just as angrily. I bit her lip—no doubt it would leave a mark—and she pulled my hair roughly in return. I felt my pants tighten even more and groaned as I pulled her even closer to me.

I needed her.

My fingers trailed under the shirt, and I heard her gasp once I grazed the bottom of her breast.

"Why aren't you wearing a bra?" I groaned painfully past her lips but she didn't answer.

Her thighs wrapped around me, and she threw her head back, letting out a soft moan.

I f*cking lost it.

"Morgan," I warned, silently cringing at how my voice cracked. "We need to stop." *If we don't stop now, we'll be doing a lot more than just kissing.*

She pushed me backwards, and I caught a small glimpse of her. Even though it was dark, I could tell she was flushed and her lip was bleeding a bit. Her eyes suddenly flashed with realization, and she stood up quickly, fanning herself.

"I-I . . . t-that," she stammered. Morgan's cheeks were bright red, and she had yet to pull her shirt down, giving me a full view of her superhero underwear. "I'm so sorry!"

"You're not wearing any pants," I coughed, trying to think of literally anything to get rid of my situation down there.

Morgan shrieked and pulled her shirt down roughly, which only managed to reveal her cleavage.

F*ck, this is a mess.

"This was a mistake," I said to her and she nodded furiously in agreement.

Although it sounded like I was trying to convince myself rather than her.

"Yeah," she stated as she inched away from me. "We were both angry. It was a rash decision, and we didn't think twice about it."

"Should we add that to the list of things we should never talk about?"

"Definitely."

After a short silence, I sighed and shook my head. "I should get going. I have work soon," I lied and pushed my way out of the restroom.

"Yeah, you have fun with that!" Morgan exclaimed awkwardly.

What the f*ck just happened?

CHAPTER FOURTEEN
If Your Dad's a Cop, Tell Him

MORGAN COLLINS

"I don't think it's a good idea to eat here," I murmured as we sat down in a booth.

My dad gave me an odd look while my mother flicked her hand dismissively. "Nonsense. We're already here," she scoffed.

I took a glance at the restaurant, looking for a certain someone.

I mean, what were the odds that he would serve us?

"Hello, my name is Mason and I'll be your waiter tonight."

I guess it was a big chance.

"Oh, look, Morgan, it's your friend!" my mom exclaimed as she waved her hand around my face as if I hadn't noticed him.

I averted my gaze from Mason's and coughed. "Hey, Mason."

We hadn't talked since that day. We avoided each other at school, and eventually things went back to the way they were before a very drunken Mason came into my room. Well, as normal as they could get with Dee poking at me to tell her what had happened.

"Morgan . . . Mr. and Mrs. . . . ." Mason was waiting for someone to fill in the spot.

This idiot never even bothered to learn my last name! I saw his dick, and he never even took the time to learn my name!

"Collins," my dad filled in and finally looked up from his phone. His nonchalant expression turned into a scowl as he took Mason in.

"Hunter," he growled.

For the first time ever, worry flashed through Mason's golden eyes. It was gone as quick as it came, but I had noticed it.

"Officer Collins, it's always a pleasure seeing you," Mason said, although I doubt it was sincere.

"You two know each other?" My mom raised her eyebrow questioningly.

"Unfortunately," my dad snarled. Mom gave Dad a look of annoyance at his short answer and sighed.

"Can I talk to you for a second, Morgan?" Mason asked, earning a suspicious look from my dad.

"Don't try anything funny," Dad warned.

"Your dad's a cop," Mason hissed once we were away from the table. "Wait, no, not just a f*cking cop, but the cop that put me in juvie, Morgan. Juvie. Why didn't you tell me?"

"I didn't think it'd be something you needed to know," I raised my eyebrow at his outburst. He sure kept a cool façade around other people, but right now he looked extremely nervous.

"Are you sh*tting me? It is when I'm the delinquent who kissed his daughter in his house. Oh, I wore his clothes, his f*cking clothes, Morga—"

I put my hand on his mouth, and he quickly shut up. Mason's eyes were wide, and he was breathing hard. Mason was never like this. He wasn't even this freaked out when he was getting his ass beat.

"Calm down, Mason. I bet my dad doesn't even hate you. He's just a bit cranky today." I tried to calm him down, but he just narrowed his eyes and pulled my hand back.

"I broke his nose," Mason stated, giving me a daring look.

"That was you?" I questioned as my brows knitted together in a frown.

75

Mason sighed and looked down at his shoes. "I was sent to juvie and my social worker had to bust me out weeks later, but to be fair he grabbed onto me first."

I pinched the bridge of my nose in frustration and shook my head. "Just take our order and ignore him. It'll be fine. He won't know."

Mason nodded slowly, then we made our way back to the booth. My dad was tapping his fingers in frustration.

"Anything to drink?" Mason mumbled. His façade was back on.

How did he do that? He was just panicking a few minutes before, and now he was calm and collected. F*cking wizard.

"Diet coke." My mom smiled and kicked my dad under the table when he refused to look at Mason.

"Coke," he grumbled.

"Same." I nodded.

Mason handed us the menus before taking off.

"I don't want you hanging out with that boy," my dad stated as he opened the menu.

"What?" I let out. I mean, I wasn't planning to hang out with him after what happened, but it was still way out of place to ban me from being friends with someone!

"Honey," my mom said warily.

"He's trouble, Ellie! He's going to ruin our daughter," he exclaimed.

My mother arched a brow but didn't take her eyes off the menu. "From what I remember, you weren't such a good influence either, Parker. I turned out just fine," she defended.

"But that's different."

I rolled my eyes and slumped in my seat. "You can't ban our daughter from hanging out with someone unless she's in danger. Mason seems like a really nice boy."

"He broke my nose," my dad grumbled angrily and crossed his arms.

76

"Here are your drinks." Mason came back with the drinks and flipped open a small notebook. "What can I get you started with tonight?"

"I'd like some tacos," my dad grumbled, not bothering to take a look at the menu.

Oh, sh*t is about to go down.

"We don't serve tacos, Officer Collin."

He stood up abruptly and looked around in annoyance. "This is bullsh*t. We're leaving."

My mom threw an apologetic look at Mason before stomping angrily after my dad. He would probably be sleeping on the couch tonight.

"I think that went pretty well." Mason nodded his head as he stuffed the notepad into his apron.

I chuckled but shook my head slowly. "Yeah, sorry about that."

I watched as the corners of his lips pulled up into a smile. He shrugged. "See you in school."

*　　*　　*

"Why did you two stop talking?" Richard sat next to me in anatomy the next day and pouted. "Did my plan not work?"

I wasn't supposed to be talking to him. I looked around and failed to spot Mason. Oh well, he wasn't here to see it.

Wait a f*cking minute, Mason didn't pay me any bills. Why the f*ck was I over here listening to him? I could talk to whoever I wanted. He could suck it.

"Maybe you've taken interest in some other boy," he winked after a prolonged amount of silence. I gave him a look.

"Mason told me about Jessica," I blurted out, "and how you always want his leftovers."

Richard's smug smile fell and his forehead puckered.

"And that's why you think I'm talking to you?"

I didn't answer. To be fair, it kind of looked that way. Why would Richard talk to me now out of nowhere after I became friends with Mason?

"That's not the reason I'm talking to you, Morgan, but I get it. You're worried for your well-being. I'll leave you alone if—"

"Why would I be worried for my well-being?" I cut off, scrunching up my nose in confusion.

"Because of what happened to Jessica . . ." Richard trailed off slowly.

"Mason told me that she stepped on the frozen lake after you left to go get some blankets," I clarified and watched as he started shaking his head.

"Morgan, Mason pushed Jessica into the lake after finding out that she was cheating on him."

CHAPTER FIFTEEN
Go to Detention with Him

"What?" I managed to spit out.

"Okay, class, we'll get started. I'm going to play this video for the entire class period so just stay quiet. If any of the administration comes in, tell them you're answering questions," Mrs. Porter said in a monotonous voice and lazily pointed at the three questions on the board.

Richard inched closer and nodded. "What Mason told you was true. I took his girl, and she didn't want to break up with him. She was looking for the right time, you know? Jessica came to my party after her and Mason got in a fight. I did leave her by the lake to get some blankets.

"When I came back, Mason was on the dock, looking down. He said Jessica said some things to him before walking into the ice, but he wouldn't tell anyone but the—"

"You're in my seat, Venice," a strained voice came from beside us.

Mason's eyes were shining with fury and both his fists were clenched.

"Why didn't you tell her the truth about Jessica? You pushed her," Richard blamed, ignoring his first statement.

"I didn't push her, and you know that. It was ruled a suicide," he spoke through gritted teeth.

This was all very f*cking interesting, but why the hell did no one notice that Richard and Mason were having a f*cking argument in the middle of the class? *Is Mrs. Porter awake? Is she dead? Oh my freaking gosh, is she dead?*

Richard snorted. "You expect me to believe that she just walked on the ice while you were there? She was happy. You might have fooled the cops, but I'm not stupid."

So Mason was there?

"Mason!" Mrs. Porter exclaimed over the video. "Sit down!"

Okay, she is fine.

Mason waved his hand dismissively at her and leaned onto the table, setting his hands next to Richard.

"Think what you want, Venice. I can give two flying f*cks about what you think of me."

"You sure had a motive to push her. You've always been jealous of me, Mason. Everyone likes me better, even Jessica."

Um, this wasn't going anywhere good. You know what was going good? F*cking Wendy's four for four special. That sh*t was mad cheap. I could go for some Wendy's right about now.

"Mason, if you don't get into a seat this instant, I will send you to detention," Mrs. Porter warned.

Again, Mason dismissed her.

"Mason, I think you should sit down," I whispered. I knew this had nothing to do with me, but he was starting to create a scene. Also, he was going to get sent to detention if he wouldn't sit down.

Mason's eyes darted towards me for the first time, and he smiled bitterly, all traces of anger leaving his face. "I think you're right, Morgan. I should sit down. Venice, get out of my seat."

"Or else what? You'll push me into a lake? We both know you're a pus—"

Before Richard could finish his sentence, Mason's fist rammed into his jaw and Richard fell back.

Mrs. Porter shrieked and a collective sound of gasps came from the students in the class.

"Mason!" I exclaimed as I went to shield Richard once I saw Mason approaching him.

"You're defending him? He's a f*cking liar!" Mason spat in disbelief. I opened my mouth to argue with him but Mrs. Porter intervened.

"All three of you, detention!" she exclaimed.

Dumb b*tch, I was only trying to help. "But—"

"Detention," she repeated more forcefully.

That was basically how we all found ourselves sitting in Room 304, glaring at the wall.

There was a passed out kid sitting in the back. The attending teacher was currently blasting funny YouTube videos on his headphones. As for Mason, Richard, and I, we were fighting the boredom that came with detention.

"You could've just gotten up from my seat," Mason said loudly, not caring if the teacher in charge heard him. Richard pressed the ice bag into his swollen eye and narrowed his other one. For the first time since I met Richard, he looked annoyed.

"You could've just admitted that you pushed Jessica," Richard spat back angrily.

"Why the f*ck would I jump in the freezing water to go get her if I had pushed her in? Kind of defeats the purpose, don't you think, sh*t for brains?"

"Whatever." Richard finally gave up and adjusted the bag on his face. "Just don't take Morgan to any lakes."

He murmured the last part, but Mason sure caught it.

"What's your deal with Morgan? Does she have flavored nipples or something that I don't know about?"

"Hey!" I cried out but was ignored by both of them.

"What's your deal with Morgan? Why did you lie about your whereabouts during Jessica's death?" Richard shot back.

Mason clenched his fist and mumbled something under his breath.

"What?" I questioned.

He grunted, "None of your f*cking business."

"Hey!" a voice came from the back. "Can all of you just shut up?"

I turned to look at the kid who was previously sleeping.

"Do you have a problem with something?" Mason turned back with a raised eyebrow. "Because if you do, I'll gladly fix it for you."

The boy's eyes widened and he shook his head quickly. "M-Mason, I didn't know. I-I," he stammered and put his head back down with a quick sorry.

"You're a b*tch, Mason."

"If you don't shut up, I'm going to shove my fist down your f*cking throat, Venice."

I shushed them loudly, earning both of their gazes. "If no one shuts up, I'm going to shove my fist up your asses."

Both of them turned around with furrowed eyebrows. "What kind of porn do you watch?" Mason asked.

I hate them both.

*   *   *

I felt my bed shift that night and sprang up, ready to slam someone in the head with . . . Well, I didn't know with what, but I was planning to hit them with something.

"Oh, it's you," I mumbled as I caught sight of Mason. "Are you drunk?"

He shook his head and looked down.

"Did you get kicked out of your house?"

"I just couldn't sleep," he murmured.

I rubbed my eyes and frowned. "What the f*ck do I look like? A group of sheep?"

"A flock," he corrected quite uselessly.

Excuse me? No one should come into my house and correct me.

"What are you doing here, Mason?" I questioned as I turned to face him.

He paused before sighing. "Do you really think I pushed her?"

"I don't know, Mason. I wasn't there," I mumbled.

I honestly didn't know what to think. I thought Richard wasn't lying, but I thought Mason wasn't either. All in all, I didn't give a single f*ck. I was just trying to graduate.

"Plus, I thought you didn't care what people thought about you," I added, yawning right after. It was 3 AM. I wanted to sleep.

"I-I don't," he defended quickly. "I just don't want Richard giving you any ideas."

"Why do you need me to believe you?" I asked after a long silence.

"I—"

The door burst open and Dee came in with my spare key in her hand.

"Hey, M, I need a place to—oh, I wasn't aware you had company."

"This is not what it looks like, Dee." I threw my hands up in defense.

"I'll crash on your couch until you're available." And with that, she shut the door.

CHAPTER SIXTEEN
Ask Him if the Rumors are True

MASON HUNTER

"Did you actually join the mob?"

I rolled my eyes at the question of Morgan's friend but chuckled nevertheless. "That one was fake," I answered as I pushed the lunch plate away from me.

Someone really needs to look into the school food.

"How about the one that said that you sold your kidney on the black market for a new pair of sneakers?" Morgan spoke up, curiosity sparking in her green eyes.

I smirked. *She is not going to believe this.*

"That one was partially true," I mumbled, pulling my shirt up and revealing a scar on my side.

"Shut the f*ck up!" the one with black hair exclaimed. "He has f*cking abs, Morgan! Abs!

Morgan rolled her eyes and shook her head. "Dee, stop." She turned back around and her eyes widened once she saw the scar. "What the f*ck? Your kidney, Mason?"

"My last foster parent had a cousin that sold sh*t on the black market. I sold mine for a truck," I finished, smirking.

Out of all the craziest rumors out there, this was the only one that was kind of true.

"You're f*cking joking," Morgan exclaimed as she let out a full blown laugh.

My heart skipped a beat.

*Wow, her laugh is so f*cking breathtak—*

I stopped myself before I could complete my thought, and my eyes widened at the sudden realization.

*F*ck, no, not again.*

"I have to go to the restroom," I stood up quickly, not bothering to stop to hear their response.

No, Mason, no, no. There is no way in hell that you're starting to crush on Morgan.

I burst into the restroom and glared at the guys that were washing their hands. "Get the f*ck out of here," I growled, causing them to scurry out.

I leaned on the sink and stared at my reflection.

You can't crush on Morgan. Last time you fell in love, someone died.

"I'm so sorry, Mason. I love you."

I shook my head as Jessica's words rang in my head.

No, I didn't like her. I just went through some tough sh*t, and she was the only one there for me. I just thought I needed to repay her.

The door suddenly flew open and a guy walked in. I had seen him a few times, but I couldn't remember his name.

He glared at me and leaned against the sink I was in front of.

"Mason, right?" he asked while he raised an eyebrow at me.

I wasn't really in the mood to chat.

"I have an understanding that you're trying to get with Morgan," he spoke with a light accent even though I hadn't answered his first question.

*Geez, man, take a f*cking hint.*

"Listen, doucheba—"

"No, you listen," he cut me off aggressively and puffed up his chest. "I need you to stay away from her."

85

He has to be joking.

"And who the f*ck are you?" I countered calmly, not bothering to change my stance.

"Dante."

I scoffed and clicked my tongue. "Who the f*ck are you to her, you stupid dick? I don't give a damn about your name."

Dante's eyes flashed with anger as he combed his fingers through his hair. "A close friend," he mumbled.

I laughed sarcastically and cocked my head to the side. "Really? Because she's never mentioned you, and I happen to talk to her a lot."

Okay, I admit I was pushing his buttons. The dickhead deserved it after coming into the restroom to try and tell me what to do.

His nostrils flared and my lips curled up into a smirk.

Again, does this girl have flavored nipples or something?

"You're after a girl that doesn't know you exist." I nodded sympathetically. "While you're thinking of her, she's busy with me."

Dante snarled and pushed me back violently. "Shut the f*ck up, Mason."

I arched my eyebrows at him and chuckled. "Are you really trying to push a guy who has a reputation for breaking noses?"

As if on cue, a few bulky guys slithered out of the bathroom stalls. Oh great, the whole soccer team was here.

"I think you're a bit too cocky, cabrón," Dante growled.

I rolled my eyes at his insult. Living a few years in a Mexican household really paid off.

"How long have those pussies been in there?" I laughed. How long had they been waiting? What if I didn't decide to come to the restroom?

One of the guys stepped forward, but I had yet to move from my initial position. I was still leaning against the sink, staring at him through the mirror. He cracked his knuckles and the rest

86

followed suit. "Come on, guys, I don't think this is a fair fight," I chuckled.

There was no way I could beat four guys, but I could have fun trying.

"¿Qué hacemos con el gringo, Dante?" another guy spoke. I believed it meant something along the lines of "What do we do with him?"

"For starters, you can watch me beat your pussy of a friend—" I smiled at him and finally stood up straight "—or you could join the fun."

All of them looked at me as if I had grown two heads.

"What?" I questioned. "Just because I'm white doesn't mean I can't understand Spanish."

They didn't answer.

"Are we going to fight or not? I'm starting to get bored," I said as I heard the bell ring.

"Crush him," Dante hissed and I wasted no time to smash my fist into the mirror. I grabbed the biggest shard and faced them. "Let's go then."

"Whoa!" the first guy exclaimed as he jumped back. "Are you f*cking crazy?"

I lifted my arms in question as I watched everyone, even Dante, take a few steps back.

"What? Was I supposed to just let four guys beat me up?" I asked, narrowing my eyes in question.

"Are you okay, man? Is everything cool at home?" Dante started, raising his hands up in surrender.

"What is this? Twenty questions?" I hissed, letting the shard smash into the floor in frustration.

"That shouldn't be the first thing you think of doing when someone wants to fight you." One of the guys shook his head in worry. "If you need help—"

I waved my hand at them, which was now starting to bleed. "Forget it," I mumbled and shoved through them. "Come back when you actually want to fight."

I walked out of the restroom and wrapped my injured hand with my sweater. Everyone had already cleared the hall.

I really need to go home.

"Hey, there you are," Morgan exclaimed from a distance and jogged towards me. "You forgot your phone."

My heart started to beat quickly as she took my hand. "Hey, are you okay?"

Get yourself together, dipsh*t.

"Y-yeah." I cursed internally when I heard myself stutter. "I just had a very strange encounter with your friend."

"What friend?" Morgan asked, a small frown had started to form on her face.

"Dante." I laughed awkwardly.

Sh*t, where was that confident Mason? Where the f*ck was the guy who was ready to shank some guy in the restroom?

She sighed. "He can be a little weird. Are you sure you're alright? You look flushed. I can take you to the nur—"

"No!" I exclaimed. "I just need to go home."

Why is she being so damn nice?

Morgan inched closer and took another look at my hand. "What happened? It looks pretty ba—"

"I said I'm fine, Morgan," I hissed at her.

Her face instantly changed and she pulled back. "Fine, b*tch. Help yourself."

Then Morgan turned on the balls of her feet and walked away.

I am so dead.

CHAPTER SEVENTEEN
Go on a Date

MORGAN COLLINS

"So, what happened with you and Mason?" I raised a brow at Dante as I took a seat next to him in English. English had never been my favorite subject, but here I was, listening to Mr. Dane as he introduced the next chapter of Fahrenheit 451 in the most monotonous voice possible.

F*cking English class.

He chuckled nervously and scratched the back of his neck. "You know, just guy stuff . . ."

The announcement suddenly came on and the principal's voice boomed loudly on the intercom.

"Sorry for the interruption, students and staff. Whoever broke the mirror in the boy's restroom should come forward or else there will be serious consequences. If the one responsible fails to comply, then I will be forced to remove all the mirrors in the boy's restrooms for everyone's safety. Thank you."

There was a collective sound of groans as the announcement finished.

"Just guy stuff, huh?" I gave him a deadpan look.

"Pinche gringo," he mumbled under his breath, then smiled nervously. "He fell."

I hummed and went back to Mr. Dane. He started to read the book again. He seemed so caught up that he didn't spare a second glance to his students, who were either asleep or on their phone.

"Anyways, do you want to go out sometime?" Dante rushed, avoiding my gaze. "You know, maybe catch a movie or something."

Wait, what?

"You mean like on a date?" I asked, surprised. I had never been asked out. Maybe it was because I looked like a ballsack or I just weirded guys out sometimes.

Whatever it was, it deprived me from dating.

"Yeah." He gave me a lopsided grin. "You're not dating Mason, right?"

"No, Mason's just a friend." The words felt foreign to me.

If you had told me a month ago that I was going to be friends with Mason, I would have probably laughed at you.

"So, are you down?"

I snapped back to reality and smiled at him.

To say this was a huge surprise was an understatement. Dante didn't really talk to any girls, not romantically anyways. He had never shown any interests in dating anyone.

Don't get me wrong, he was cute. Big brown eyes, lean body, tan skin, and that extremely hot accent could have any girl swooning. Why was I thinking so much about it? A really hot guy is asking me out!

"Yeah, sure." I beamed at him.

His face brightened up and he started to scribble up his number on a sheet of paper. "This is my number. Send me your address, and I'll pick you up on Friday."

I nodded and took the piece of paper, shoving it in my pocket before turning back to the teacher.

"Hey, b*tch," Dee greeted as she hovered over my locker once class had ended. "Why do you have that look on your face?"

90

Dee arched her brows at the piece of paper sticking from my pocket and went to grab it. "Someone's digits."

She gasped dramatically. "Are they Mason's? Richard's? Ohhh, girl—"

"Dante's," I cut her off as I reached for the paper. "We're going on a date this Friday."

"Dante?" she said doubtfully. "Since when did you talk to Dante?"

I picked a few books and shut my locker before turning to her. "What? You don't think he's cute?"

"No, no, he's a total babe—"

"Talking about me again," Richard suddenly interrupted as he put an arm around me.

"About Dante," Dee clarified as I shrugged off Richard's arm. "Morgan and him are going on a date."

"Dante?" Richard murmured. "What about Mason?"

What about Mason?

"What about me?" Mason also intercepted, sipping on a carton of apple juice.

Where the f*ck do all these people come from?

"She's going on a date with Dante," Richard pointed out, causing Mason to spit out his drink at Richard in surprise.

"Classy," Richard hissed and wiped the apple juice off his face.

"Dante?" Mason exclaimed, ignoring Richard's annoyed glare. "Since when have you been lovey dovey with Dante?"

"My point exactly!" Dee waved her arms around.

I sighed. "Dante's cute and funny, and he asked me out, so let it go," I scowled at all of them and took off to my next class.

"You can't go out with Dante." Mason caught up to me.

"Why not?"

Mason shoved himself in front of me, making me stop all together. "Because I said so," he ordered lamely and I rolled my eyes.

"Don't make me laugh, Mason." I chuckled sarcastically as I tried to step around him. Unfortunately, he blocked the path to my class.

He let out a breath and glanced at me softly. "Please?"

His puppy dog eyes almost had me, but luckily, I was a stubborn ass b*tch.

"No."

"Geez, Mason, try to contain your jealousy." Richard walked towards us but Dee was no longer him.

"I'm not jealous," Mason growled. "I just don't like Dante."

I glanced at his fist, which was starting to recover, and then back at him. "Just how you don't like Richard?"

Richard nodded his head and pursed his lips. "She's got a point."

I was starting to think that Mason just didn't want me to have a love life.

"Shut the f*ck up, pinhead," Mason shot back and then turned to me. "Fine, go out with Dante. See if I give a f*ck."

"Fine, I will."

The rest of the week went by quickly, and before I knew it, I was patting my frizzy hair awkwardly in Dante's car. I watched him pull up to the restaurant.

He had to be f*cking kidding me.

"Here?" I raised my eyebrow at the restaurant.

I had actually bothered to do my makeup and put on something nice. Who knew? Maybe I would actually hit it off with Dante.

"It'll be fun, linda." He winked at me and hopped off the car before opening my door. "After you, hermosa."

Dante speaking Spanish was the hottest thing ever. He could have been calling me a wh*re and I would still be swooned.

I smiled and followed him into a booth.

"Hey, can you take our order?" Dante waved with a smirk.

"Good afternoon, can I offer you something to f*cking choke on?"

CHAPTER EIGHTEEN
Lick Him

"Mason, you work here?" Dante exclaimed in delight as he sanded his hands together.

I pursed my lips suspiciously at this. Why was Dante so excited to see Mason? Why did Mason look like he had just swallowed a dick? And why didn't they serve tacos in this place?

I put the menu down and smiled at Mason, although he was too busy glaring at Dante to even notice me.

"Save the act, dipsh*t. You know I work here," he mumbled as he finally turned to look at me.

"You finally look decent," he noted. Mason almost hissed at me, then turned back to the notepad.

"Can we get another waiter? You know, someone who doesn't treat customers like trash," I growled at his attitude, and in result, he rolled his golden eyes, letting out an exasperated breath in the process. I was getting so sick of his stupid mood swings. One day he was my friend, the other I was touching his dick, and all of a sudden, he's pissed because I wanted to go on one date.

"Or you can move to a table that isn't mine," Mason shot back, smiling bitterly at the both of us.

He was trying to get a rise out of me, and it was f*cking working.

I opened my mouth to swear the living sh*t out of him, but Dante spoke up before I could.

"Whoa, Mason, what's up your ass? Are you a little jealous?" Dante chimed in with a light chuckle as he peeked at the menu.

"This—" he gestured towards Dante and me with his hand "—won't last a week, and do you know why?"

"Why?" Dante arched his brow as I narrowed my eyes.

"Because she likes me."

I froze at Mason's choice of words.

"Like you?" I questioned and gave him a look.

"Don't act like you don't. It's more than obvious," Mason pressed as he got too close for my liking.

I wanted to laugh in his face and tell him he was delusional, but the words wouldn't pass my lips.

He smirked at my silence and pulled away, shrugging. "And this assh*le tried to beat me up in the restroom with his soccer team. He asked me to stop talking to you and flaunted the fact that you guys were going on a date as if you were some competition."

That would explain why Dante looked so smug when we first got here.

"That's not true!" Dante quickly denied as he shook his head.

"He told me he only wants you just because you started hanging out with me. He wants to win a competition that doesn't even exist," Mason continued as he scowled at Dante who returned it back.

"Is this true?" I raised an eyebrow.

"Not all of it! Morgan, I swear," he pleaded as Mason snorted.

"I tried to warn you in the hallway, Morgan. You just pissed me off when you didn't listen, and I figured it would be best to let you figure it out by yourself," Mason stated.

I stood up and tried to swallow the lump in my throat. I did my makeup! I pulled this f*cking new dress out of my damn closet for this. I felt my eyes start to tear up, but I refused to let any of it fall.

Mom didn't raise a b*tch.

"Morgan, wait, mierda," Dante started but I put my hand up to stop him.

"I'll catch a cab. Don't worry about it. Go home," I mumbled before throwing a grateful look at Mason and stomping off.

The click of my window that night woke me up, but I didn't bother turning around. I already knew who it was.

"Hey, Morgan," he spoke softly as I felt the bed shift.

I finally turned and saw Mason, who still had his waiter uniform, cap, and everything. "Were you crying?" he questioned and I could've sworn that regret sparked in his golden orbs.

But regret for what? Telling me the truth? Something wasn't right.

"No." I winced at how my voice sounded and rubbed my eyes. They were probably swollen.

"I'm sorry," Mason mumbled, and for the first time in history, he looked uncomfortable.

"What for?" I asked.

There was a short pause as if he was debating on something. Then, he shook his head. "I don't know. Isn't that what people are supposed to say when someone is sad?" he answered.

I shrugged.

This had to be the most awkward thing in the whole planet. My heart fluttered when he nearly closed the space between us, leaving only a few inches.

"Can I tell you something?" Mason suddenly asked. His eyes zeroed in on mine, and I felt my heart stop.

Why is he so close? Can't he tell me something from afar?

"Y-yeah," I choked out.

His eyes flickered to my lips for a few seconds and I gulped. "You have something in your teeth."

96

My hand went to cover my mouth at what seemed like the speed of light and I pulled back. "Mason," I cried out.

"What?" His lips were set in a straight line, but I could hear the humor behind the words.

What an assh*le.

"I'm just kidding, f*ckface. So gullible." He rolled his eyes.

"Yeah, well, you have something on your lip," I shot back, not really knowing where this was going.

"Oh yeah? Why don't you lick it off?" Mason suggested and then smirked at my silence. "That's what I thought."

Before I could regret it, I leaned forward and licked the corner of his lip.

We both froze and stared at each other with wide eyes.

I can't believe I did that.

"Mason, oh God, I'm so sorry. I didn't meant to—"

He let out a groan as he closed the distance between us once again and pecked the corner of my lips.

I felt my cheeks heat up. "Don't apologize, f*ckface," he mentioned and stood up. "I have to go. I have to meet up with the social worker and my biological parents tomorrow," Mason murmured as he rubbed my head. "Good night."

"Are you actually giving them a chance?" My face brightened up. The thought of Mason finally leaving that sh*thole was the best news I had heard so far.

He was such a good friend even though he wanted people to think otherwise. He deserved way more than what he had.

"I figured you were right. I can't hold a grudge forever," he mumbled the last part but I caught it.

I smirked. "Can you say that again? I didn't really catch it."

"Don't push it."

CHAPTER NINETEEN
Just be Friends

MASON HUNTER

"The DNA test came back positive," my social worker, Kathy, nodded as she passed the papers around. "Now, you have to understand that you can't take Mason until he's officially eighteen."

"Which is in a few days," Ronald, my birth father, nodded as he gave Olivia a quick side hug.

"My birthday is in July," I clarified, creasing my brow at all of them.

"Well, we couldn't quite find your actual birthday, so we made one up, but hospital records say that you were born on April 18th," Kathy stated as a matter of fact and looked back at Olivia and Ronald. "Does that sound okay?"

They both nodded.

"Kathy," Diana interrupted. "Don't you think it will affect Mason if he just gets up and leaves? He has to at least finish school here!"

I almost laughed at the fake ass frown she had plastered on her wrinkled face as if she actually cared. She had never given a rat's ass about me.

"We can move!" Olivia exclaimed loudly as she nodded her head eagerly.

"What?" Alexandra scowled as she stood up. "I already gave him weekends! Now you want me to give him the last few months of my junior year too?"

Alexandra, better known as Lexi, was my actual birth sister. She was extremely spoiled, wore short skirts, and pranced around with designer bags.

But at least she bothered to show up as opposed to her twin brother, Alexander.

"There seems to be a conflict here," Robert pointed out gruffly as he gave Kathy a look. "We can keep Mason for a few more months. It won't be a problem, right, Mason?"

"Mmm-hmm," I hummed in agreement, not really caring what was agreed on. I would be unwanted in both homes. It was all the same to me.

"I agree," Kathy murmured and continued with a string of words that I decided to tune out.

I should've brought Morgan along. Maybe then I wouldn't be so bored.

I shook my head subtly and swore internally.

Morgan was such a good person. Maybe I shouldn't have lied to her about Dante. I couldn't keep controlling her life. We were just friends. I shouldn't intervene in her love life.

If she wanted to date Dante, then she could date Dante! Why did I care so much about it?

You like her, dumbass.

I shook my head at my inner voice.

Yeah, I thought Morgan was cute. She made me happy when she wasn't annoying, but she deserved way better than me. I needed a new beginning, and that would start by getting over this f*cking stupid "crush" I had on Morgan.

"We'll move to town anyways! Even if it's just temporary, we'll be here for Al—err, Mason just in case he needs us." Olivia's voice brought me back to reality.

Lexi scoffed and went back to her phone while the social worker nodded. "That's fine," Kathy murmured.

The rest of the day flew by quickly, and before I knew it, it was Monday.

"Can we talk?" I heard Lacey say as she tapped my shoulder slowly.

I was still trying to point Morgan out of the crowd. I needed to tell her about Dante and get over this whole Morgan-you-can't-go-out-with-this-guy phase.

"Mason," Lacey said again. I finally turned to her, giving her an insincere smile.

"What's up?"

"We had sex," she pointed out the obvious. She looked at me expectantly as if she were waiting for me to have a sudden epiphany.

"Yeah . . ." I creased my brow at her choice of words.

"I thought, you know, things would be different," Lacey frowned and played with the hem of her cheerleader skirt.

"Are you free this Saturday?" Lacey was hot, but she wasn't really my type. She was a distraction though. Maybe I could f*ck my way out of liking Morgan.

Her eyes lit up and she nodded.

"How about I pick you up at eight?"

Lacey smiled. Her cheeks flushed before she stood on her tippy-toes and pecked my cheek.

It lacked the rush I got when Morgan kissed me, but it was a start.

"Mason!"

I could recognize that annoying ass high-pitched voice anywhere.

"I better go," Lacey excused herself and smiled at me again. "See you on Saturday."

I winked at her and made sure to wear my cocky façade. *No more "nice boy" when dealing with Morgan. You're going to get over her.*

"You," Morgan hissed as she jabbed her finger on my chest. "Did you lie about Dante?"

I assumed Dante had snitched already. *B*tch.*

"Yeah." I shrugged, amused by the spark of anger that lit up in her green eyes.

"You can't just mess with my life, Mason! I—"

"I know," I cut her off. "I promise not to give a single f*ck about you in the future."

That's right, Mason. You don't care about her. You don't like her.

She grabbed the collar of my shirt and pulled me close. I couldn't help but notice how her knuckles grazed my chest, sending me into a fit of nervousness.

Oh f*ck, Mason. You don't have this. She has you wrapped around her fingers.

"Do you think I'm playing?" she whispered as the tardy bell went off. "Mason, you're a good friend, but you're not my dad or my boyfriend for that matter to be telling me who the f*ck I can go out with!"

"I know," I admitted, prying her fingers from my shirt before I lost my sanity. "I have a date this Saturday. I'll be someone else's problem, and you can start focusing on what's his face."

She deserves better. She deserves better. She deserves better, I kept repeating it in my head. I had baggage. I was all kinds of f*cked up, and my life was a f*cking mess. She was better off with Dante.

Something flashed in her eyes, but it was gone as soon as it appeared. "Oh," she mumbled, "with who?"

"Lacey," I stated. "So we can stay friends, right? No more dick situations or kissing?"

"Yeah," she agreed quietly as she took my hand. "Friends."

I ripped my hand away from hers as quickly as possible, scowling at the tingles that shot up my arm.

"Good."

This is the right thing to do, right?

101

*   *   *

"I should be happy that he's someone else's problem, right?"

Richard and Dee both shared a look and then gazed at Mason, who was sitting at the popular table next to Lacey.

"He looks bored out of his mind," Richard pointed out.

"Do you think he just wants to f*ck her?"

I felt a rush of jealousy at the pit of my stomach and furrowed my eyebrows.

Why was I jealous? I should be happy that Mason found a girl he could trust. I could go out with Dante again. No more interruptions.

"Maybe," Dee said as she picked her carrots.

"Well, I hope she's worth it," I blurted out and Dee hopped up instantly.

"You like him! I knew it!"

"What? I don't like Mason." I scoffed as I turned to her.

"Denial's always the first step." Richard pointed at me with his spork.

"I'm not in denial," I growled at both of them and slumped into my seat.

"But you think he's hot, and you don't like the fact that someone else is taking your bad boy." Dee raised her eyebrow at my silence.

"Dee?"

"Yes?"

"Shut the f*ck up."

CHAPTER TWENTY
Go to the Carnival

Dee huffed and hit the steering wheel in frustration, narrowing her eyes on the road. "Where do I park?" The f*cking carnival was in town, so here I was with Dee looking for a parking space.

"Maybe we should just go home," I suggested hopefully.

Don't get me wrong, I loved the carnival as much as the next girl, but the whole town was going to be there. Plus, I was wearing my new shoes, they might get dirty.

"Maybe you should just f*ck off," Dee shot back, making me raise my arms in surrender.

"B*tch," I mumbled.

Dee's face instantly brightened up as soon as she caught sight of a parking space. "B*tch, I—hey!" she exclaimed as a car rushed into the space before she could get there.

"There's a lot of parking space over there," I pointed out as I flicked my chin towards the very dark area that had little to no cars.

"Uh-huh," Dee denied, shaking her head furiously. "I am not leaving my car there. Someone is going to break into my car."

I narrowed my eyes at her and scoffed. "Dee, no one is going to break into your broke ass car."

"At least I have a car, dumb wh*re," she grumbled and I nodded in acknowledgement.

I mean, she wasn't wrong.

After a bit of arguing, Dee hesitantly decided to park her car, and we walked into the carnival. "What do you want to get on first?" Dee's eyes twinkled in excitement as she looked at all the rides. I opened my mouth to respond but was quickly cut off by her.

"You know what? Get in line for the ferris wheel while I go pee!" she ordered before she scurried off.

I sighed but made my way to the ferris wheel anyways. I knew better than to piss Dee off. I was surprised to find that the line was very short considering that the place was packed. I guess everyone went to all the good rides.

"Hey." I heard someone say. I peeked from my phone to see a boy, maybe around sixteen years old, pointing at the ferris wheel. "Would you mind riding with me? I don't want to be all alone."

He ran a hand through his blond hair, and I furrowed my brows. There was something about him that was so familiar.

"I'm actually waiting for someone." I smiled apologetically and he returned the smile.

"Ah." He nodded. "My name's Alexander, but everyone calls me Xander."

There was a snort from the front of the line. It was a girl who I assumed was related to "Xander" due to their facial similarities. She was wearing a tight shirt matched with a mini skirt.

"No one calls you that," she admitted and turned back to another boy.

"Shut up, Lexi," Alexander growled and turned back to me. "Sorry about that."

"It's fine." I chuckled and shoved my phone in my back pocket.

"So, who are you with?" Alexander shone a lopsided smile, and I couldn't help but notice that he was really attractive.

Mason!

I finally realized. He reminded me so much of f*cking Mason. The golden eyes were so much alike Mason's.

"My best friend," I answered and arched my brow. "Do you know Mason Hunter?"

He shook his head slowly and frowned. "Sorry, I don't think I do."

"Last seat!" the man shouted as he gestured at Alexander.

Alexander walked up and said something to the man.

"Is anyone willing to ride with this boy?" the man exclaimed loudly, causing Alexander to wince.

A girl came forward and gave him a smile, then joined him in the seat.

"Lacey?" I mumbled. I could've sworn I saw a flash of red hair.

"What's up, f*ckface?" a deep voice rumbled from my side.

"What are you doing here?"

"I'm taking Lacey on a date." Mason shrugged as we watched the wheel move. "Who are you here with?"

I ignored his question and pointed forward. "She got in with another guy."

"Yeah," Mason said as he put his hands in his pockets. "That was my brother. Lacey felt bad that he was going alone."

"He said he didn't know anyone named Mason," I pointed out.

A smirk made its way onto his face, and he shook his head. "He knows me by Alessandro. Why are you asking around for me?"

"I—he looked like you," I said lowly, hating that a blush made its way onto my face.

F*ck me. I hated to admit it, but I was almost sure that I had a crush on Mason. If the blush on my face didn't give it up, then my stuttering would.

"Yeah," Mason mumbled sarcastically and I could tell he was trying to hold back a smile.

What if you just tell him?

105

I shook my head. How would Mason even react? He was on a date with Lacey, and I was kind of dating Dante.

It's just a crush. It'll pass.

"Morgan, do you picture a future with someone like Dante?" Mason suddenly asked as he looked down at his shoes.

I shrugged.

Dante was a nice guy, but I didn't picture myself marrying him. I didn't feel like he was the one.

"He's alright," I said, not quite answering his question.

"I mean, would you prefer him over someone whose life was f*cked?" he asked again.

Why is he asking me this?

I turned to look at him, only to find him still staring at his shoes. "Stability is good," I decided. "Why?"

"I need help with making a decision," Mason mumbled but didn't mention anything else.

"What—"

"I'm back. The line was long as fuc—am I interrupting anything?" Dee said as she eyed both of us suspiciously.

"Nope," Mason answered before I could and sent us a fake smile. "I have to get back to the Warrens before Lacey and Alexander get back."

I nodded and Dee waved her fingers at him. "Bye!"

"Is it just me, or does he look troubled?" I told Dee. She shrugged her shoulders.

"Doesn't he always?"

Good point.

"Hey guys, what are the odds that I'd see you here?" Richard chuckled as he stood beside us.

"Is the whole f*cking school here?" I exclaimed and threw my hands in the air.

Richard raised his hands and backed up a bit. "Okay, chill."

I needed a break.

CHAPTER TWENTY-ONE
Tell Him to Disappear

> *"Once upon a time an angel and a devil fell in love. It did not end well."*
>
> -Daughter of Smoke and Bone

MORGAN COLLINS

"Hey."

I turned from my locker and watched Alexander smile at me.

I eyed him and raised a brow at his clothes but responded anyway, "Hey, you go here?"

He stood out like a sore thumb. Unlike most of us who were rocking the school uniform, he was wearing a pair of slacks and a button-up shirt. He looked expensive.

"Just transferred from Pacifica High." He shrugged and I nodded.

Figures. Rich boy, rich school.

"You transferred from Pacifica High to this dump? At the end of the year?" I couldn't help but arch my brows at him in pure confusion.

Pacifica was one of the best schools in the state.

Alexander narrowed his golden eyes and scoffed. "Yeah, family issues."

Before I could say anything else, he was shoved into the lockers roughly.

"Hey, pretty boy." I recognized the voice as Jules Garcia, one of the guys on the soccer team. I didn't really interact with him much. Then again, he was always suspended.

"You look like you have money," one of his minions teased. I didn't really know who the f*ck he was.

"You wanna give us a few bucks?" Jules said, clicking his tongue after.

Alexander looked terrified. I couldn't blame him. Pacifica High wasn't famous for bullies.

"I wouldn't mess with him if I were you," I taunted but didn't move from my spot. "That's Mason's little brother."

"Mason's an only child," another minion said as he shook his head. "There's no way they're related."

"You can take the chance and find out." I shrugged and crossed my arms.

Jules looked at the other guys back and forth before giving Alexander one last push.

"I think she's lying," one said.

The bell rang, signaling the start of the fifth period. The halls soon filled with rushed students.

"Hey, what the f*ck are you doing?"

I turned, hoping to spot Mason, but instead I saw Dante, rushing his way towards us.

"¿Qué estas haciendo, pendejo?" Dante growled as he pulled Jules off of Alexander.

Jules looked like a deer caught in headlights as he started mumbling rapidly in Spanish.

"Who's Mason?" Alexander whispered from my side. I forgot that he knew him by another name.

"Your brother. He's known as Mason around here."

"You mean Alessandro? How did you know we're related?"

I responded with a shrug. "He told me."

109

They walked off, leaving Dante, Alexander, and I standing in the halls.

"Sorry about that," Dante murmured bashfully as he scratched the back of his neck. "Jules is just having some trouble at home."

Alexander nodded. "My brother's a big deal here, huh?"

"He can get a little scary," I answered. Alexander didn't ask further and watched as the last student entered the classroom. "I gotta go. It was nice seeing you though."

The late bell rang and I smiled at Dante. "Well, that's my cue," I pointed out. "See you in English?"

"Wait," Dante came out as he gripped my wrist to stop me from leaving. "I need to talk to you."

I had been dreading this. After sadly realizing that I had a crush on Mason, I was scared of what I would tell Dante.

"I don't know if you want to go to prom together," he licked his lips.

Oh no, how do I let him down easy?

"Dante . . . I don't think this is working."

He let out a relieved sigh and smiled. "Oh, thank f*cking God. I didn't know how to tell you."

"What?" I managed to sputter out.

*I am amazing. What the f*ck does he mean?*

"Look, you're great and cute. I admit that I've been crushing on you since junior year, but you weren't really what I was expecting," he said as he gave me a small squeeze of encouragement. "But we can still be friends."

I nodded, returning his friendly smile. "Yeah, friends."

"I have to go. I'll see you later." Dante sent me a wink before turning the other way.

Well, that was easier than I thought.

I held my clothes and made my way to the gym. Coach was going to f*cking kill me for showing up late.

110

A quiet moan caught my attention halfway through the gym and I halted.

Ignore it. Keep going. That wasn't your f*cking business.

Another moan came and I realized it was coming from the hallway, meaning I would have to go through it to get to the gym.

"F*ck me," I murmured and hesitantly kept walking.

*Who the f*ck are making out in school? F*cking dumb ass kids with their dumbass—*

I let out a gasp as I watched Mason shoved his tongue down Nora's throat. Nora was a small senior who wore glasses too big for her face and was bound to be our class's valedictorian. The last person you'd expect to be making out with bad boy, Mason Hunter.

Mason opened his eyes and caught my gaze, winking at me before turning back to the task at hand.

I felt a pang of jealousy rush through my gut, but I walked past them anyways.

*What the f*ck happened to Lacey?*

I thought about Mason and Nora the rest of the day, and when night came, the thought wouldn't let me go to sleep.

"Morgan." I heard my window open and close. I didn't need to turn around to know who it was.

Why do I keep leaving my window open?

"I can't sleep," he said again, noticing I was awake too.

"Good for you," I murmured and sat up. "What the f*ck do you want me to do about it?"

"What's up with you?" He frowned.

I sighed. "You were kissing Nora," I stated.

He raised his eyebrows. "Yeah, I know. I broke up with Lacey."

There was a short silence.

"You're not jealous, are you?" Instead of the mocking tone he always used, there was disgust laced in his words.

This was wrong. Why was Mason acting like this?

111

"No," I lied as I turned to look down at my shoes.

"Good. I could never see you like that."

I scoffed. "Says the guy who kissed me twice."

Mason leaned over and narrowed his eyes, a smirk making its way onto his chiseled face. "I kiss everyone. You're not special."

He was being cold. This wasn't Mason. This was the facade he showed everyone, but I knew him. What was he up to?

Whatever it was, it still made my blood boil.

I hissed. "You're a f*cking failure, Mason. I don't know why anyone would even go for you." I didn't even mean it. I was just angry, and to be honest, a bit butthurt that he didn't like me.

"And you're not even that hot, Morgan. I don't know why you're so sure I'm even attracted to you. I just keep you around because you're so good at doing sh*t for me, so why don't you run along to your 'stable' boyfriend because I wouldn't want a disgusting—"

I lunged at him, not caring if my parents heard. I punched him and something told me he was letting me before I narrowed my eyes.

"I don't ever want to see you again. You come into my room one more time, and I will tell my dad."

Mason chuckled bitterly and rolled his eyes. "Be careful what you wish for, Morgan."

"Get the f*ck out of my room."

"Gladly."

CHAPTER TWENTY-TWO
Talk to the Cops

"You cannot save everyone. Some people are going to destroy themselves no matter how much you try to help them."
-Bryant the Gill

"There are cops everywhere," Dee pointed out upon setting foot in the school.

"I see that." I nodded as I watched my father speak to the principal. "I'll be right back."

I rushed past a couple of kids who were just as confused as us and stopped next to my father. "Hey, Dad, what's going on?"

"You can't question students without their parental supervision," Mrs. Vanderwall reassured as she moved her hands around frantically. "I understand the situation, Officer—"

"Then call their parents," my dad pushed as he handed her a list. "This is a serious case."

Mrs. Vanderwall nodded and finally took off with the list. My dad sent a look to his partner before turning to me. "Sweetie, you need to go to class. I'm working."

"Actually, sir," Officer Garret interrupted, "she's the first one on the list."

My dad sighed but led me towards an office. Officer Garret followed suit and closed the door behind him.

"We are going to ask you a series of questions about Mason Hunter. Please answer as best as you can," my dad started as he sat on a chair and set down a manila folder on the desk.

"What is going on?"

"When was the last time you saw Mason Hunter?" my dad asked after pressing a button on a tape recorder, completely ignoring my last question.

My mind fled to Saturday at midnight, when Mason and I exchanged some harsh words. Or was it later?

I hadn't seen him since then. It was now Monday. I was just hoping to apologize or ask him why he was being such a big dickhead.

"Saturday," I answered truthfully as they shared another look. "What is this all about?"

"May I talk to you men for a second?" Vanderwall burst in and both men walked outside before my dad pressed another button on the tape recorder.

My hands immediately flew to the folder, and I didn't hesitate to open it.

MASON HUNTER/ALESSANDRO WARREN
D.O.B: APRIL 18, 2000
STATUS: MISSING
LAST SEEN: FRIDAY AFTERNOON
SUSPECTS: N.A.
POSSIBLE WITNESSES: MORGAN COLLINS, RICHARD VENICE.
MEDICAL RECORD: DIAGNOSED WITH DEPRESSION, ANXIETY, ANGER ISSUES (2016, Dr. Roman)

I slapped the folder close and tried to keep up with the questions in my head.

Mason is f*cking missing? His birthday is today? Why are Richard and I the only possible witnesses? How come he never told me he had depression? How does he hide it so well?

My father and Officer Garret walked back in. Dad had a harsh scowl on his face.

"That woman is a pain," my dad murmured as Garret nodded his head.

"Tell me about it."

They both sat back on the desk and pressed the 'play' button.

"State your name, age, and relationship with Mason Hunter." My dad nodded.

"Morgan Collins. Seventeen. We were friends." I gulped, the thought of Mason missing finally registering in my head.

Were? Are. We are friends. He's fine, I tried to assure myself.

"How well do you know Mason?"

"We were close," I said even though it sounded more like a question rather than a statement.

"You said the last time you saw Mason was on Saturday?"

I nodded as my dad's face contorted into an expression of disappointment.

I bet he didn't want me involved in this, but here I was in the middle of the sh*t storm.

"Can you give a verbal confirmation?"

"Yes, the last time I saw him was on Saturday."

"What time and place would that be?"

I swallowed and debated on whether to tell the truth or not. There was no way I would get out of this alive if I told the truth, but what if it helped Mason?

"Around midnight," I said lowly and hesitated for a bit before continuing, "in my room."

My dad threw me a look that said we're talking about this later but continued with the questions.

"Mason Hunter is missing, and so far, you are the last one to see him. Is there anyone who may have wanted to hurt Mason?"

I shook my head, the news finally registering in my head. I swallowed the lump in my throat as I shook my head. "Not that I know of."

"Does Mason have any suicidal tendencies?"

"Be careful what you wish for, Morgan."

The words rang in my head, and I clenched my fist, not caring if my nails dug into the skin of my palms.

Mason was always angry. It wasn't common for him to show vulnerability. I was sure he wasn't alright with a lot of things but depression? Could it have anything to do with Jessica? Or maybe living in foster care?

Had my words finally driven him to suicide?

I shook my head. "No, he never talked about it," I finally answered.

"Is there anything that you think could have triggered Mason to leave or commit suicide?"

"I—" I choked out.

He's okay. He's strong.

I told him I never wanted to see him again.

"His foster parents are abusive," I said as my dad nodded and scribbled a few words on a paper.

*And I basically told him to f*ck off.*

"Anyone else that knows Mason well enough besides Richard Venice?"

I shook my head. "Probably no one."

"That is all for now."

*   *   *

"What the f*ck was Mason doing in your room so late?" my dad growled as he paced in front of me when I got home that afternoon. "You were the last person to see him, Morgan. Nobody else saw him on Friday."

I stayed silent and looked down at my fingers, nervously fiddling with them.

"Do you know how bad that makes you look?"

"I don't know where he is," I murmured truthfully.

What if he is dead? What if they never find him?

"What was the last thing he told you?"

My mom frowned and crossed her arms. She would always defend me, but she couldn't help me this time.

"I told him that I never wanted to see him again, then he left. I think he ran away," I told him as I looked up.

He sighed and sat next to me. "He didn't take his truck. He didn't quit his job or pick up his check. He just disappeared, and the last person who saw him was you."

"I know how fond you are of him," my mother said as she kneeled in front of me. "I'm sure he's fine."

"I don't know. That kid sure knows how to piss people off. He could be lying in a ditch some—"

"Parker!" my mother exclaimed as she glared at him.

My dad threw her an apologetic look. "Let's just hope we find him alive," he said.

Alive.

I sighed and held back tears. "Yeah," I agreed.

"You just had to go around looking for trouble. I don't get it. Why even become friends with a boy like him, Morgan?" my dad pondered as he shook his head.

I shrugged. I honestly didn't know why I had been so persistent to be his friend. "I don't know. Maybe I wanted to save him from all the problems in his life. I think I just wanted to help him."

That and my stubborn ass wouldn't leave him alone. I was sure he wouldn't be missing if I didn't bother him.

117

My mom let out an exasperated breath. "You can't save someone who doesn't want to be saved."

Did Mason ever want to be saved? I mean, he always pushed me away. Maybe he just wanted to be alone.

"I know your friend is missing and you need some time, but there will be serious consequences." My dad pointed at me accusingly and raised a brow.

"But for now, get some sleep, kiddo."

CHAPTER TWENTY-THREE
Ruin His Escape Plan

"The cops are getting pretty serious about Mason," Richard remarked as he took a seat beside Dee and me.

School had gotten kind of hectic since Mason's disappearance. Everyone was talking about him like they knew him. Many girls—including Lacey—were roaming the halls with tears rolling down their cheeks.

I had tried to bottle up everything and just pretended it wasn't happening, but it wasn't working out so well.

"No sh*t Sherlock, someone's missing," Dee emphasized as she shook her head. "It's been a week. It's getting kind of serious."

Richard scoffed and took a bite out of his apple, speaking with his mouth full. "Nothing happened to him. The dickhead just ran away."

"How do you know?" I came up, hoping there was truth behind his words.

There were a lot of theories going around. None of them were nice.

"I just know Mason." He shrugged and took another bite from his apple.

"You know where he is," Dee said, narrowing her eyes.

"No, I don't," Richard shot back as he shook his head. "But if I did, I would tell the cops. I'm tired of seeing everyone crying. They don't even know Mason."

"Mason! Oh my God!" There was a loud shriek that caused the whole cafeteria to turn towards Lacey.

Her manicured hands were wrapped around her phone, and there were tears strolling down her face.

"Where are you, baby? Oh God, I'm so sorry we broke up," she continued in between hiccups. Before I knew what I was doing, I stood up and started walking towards the crowd of people that started to form around her.

"Of course!" Lacey exclaimed. "Just tell me where it is, I'll take it to them—hey!"

My hands took a mind of their own and pried the phone from her hand, ignoring her protest.

"Mason?" I spoke into the phone.

"Who is this?" It was him. I could recognize his voice anywhere.

"You're alive," I breathed out before realizing his initial question. "It's Morgan."

"Morgan," he spat, venom lacing his tone. "Can you put Lacey on the phone?"

"Where are you? Are you coming back? There are cops looking for you." I sat down, swatting away all the stares.

"Oh, I thought you never wanted to see me again," Mason spoke with a bitter tone.

"I didn't mean it! Is that why you're gone?"

I could practically imagine him rolling his golden eyes. "The world doesn't revolve around you, f*ckface. Put Lacey on the f*cking phone. I don't have your time—"

The phone was ripped from my grasp, and I looked up to see my dad.

"Mason Hunter?" Pause. "You need to come home, son. There are people who are seriously worried about you and—"

120

My dad stared at the phone. "Garret, tell the judge we need a warrant to search Diana and Robert Olsen's home." He turned to Lacey. "I'll need to confiscate this just in case he calls back, and you—" he pointed at me "—stay out of this."

"What happened?" Lacey questioned. "I have the right to know. I'm his girlfriend!"

I held the urge to mention they broke up and looked at my dad expectantly, waiting for an answer.

"The boy didn't run away," he said before walking away with Lacey's phone.

I turned to Lacey and held her shoulders. "Lacey, what did he tell you?" I pressured.

She narrowed her eyes. "Why should I tell you?"

"Lacey, this is so much bigger than you and me," I said. Everyone was starting to go back to their seats.

She opened her mouth and sighed. "Fine."

*　　*　　*

MASON HUNTER

I received another blow to the face and resisted the urge to cry out.

That one f*cking hurt.

"Who the f*ck did you call?" Winnie growled, spitting in the process.

"Pizza Hut. I was getting hungry," I said, a smirk making its way onto my face.

Winnie grunted as he put his hand on both sides of the chair. "I'm not going to ask again. Who the f*ck did you call?"

"Ghostbusters." I smiled, shining the teeth he hadn't already kicked out. I was going to need a long trip to the dentist if I ever survived this.

"You're a f*cking pain in my ass," he exclaimed. "I am going to kill Robert."

I didn't know what kind of deal Winnie and Robert made, but it had ended in putting a bag over my head in the middle of the night. I was then shipped to Winnie's house, where he held a very illegal drug business.

"He promised me a f*cking dealer. Someone who would obey orders," Winnie hissed. "Instead I got a dumb f*cking teenager who won't shut up."

I assumed Robert wanted to make good use of me. Seeing as he wouldn't get any foster care checks anymore, he did the most logical thing a human being could do—he f*cking sold me.

But that was only an assumption. I didn't know where the f*ck I was or who the f*ck I was dealing with. I didn't even know this guy's name. I just decided to call him Winnie.

"Life's tough." I shrugged, flashing him a bloody smile. "But at least we have each other."

Winnie glared and shifted, giving me a full peek of his beer belly. F*cking Winnie the Pooh looking ass.

"You better not have called the cops or I'll kill you," he growled.

Of course, I wasn't f*cking dumb. Calling the cops would make a huge f*cking deal. Winnie would hear the sirens and kill me before they stepped in.

"So, when are you going to get me out of your creepy basement? It's getting lonely down here." I pouted and raised my hands, struggling due to the fact that my wrists were tied.

"Who did you call?" he continued, narrowing his eyes again.

I was starting to get frustrated with him. "Your mom," I replied lamely.

He pushed his fist into my stomach, and I couldn't help but cough up the little contents I had in my stomach. "If you wanted to make me gag, you could have done it some other way," I hinted jokingly in a strained voice.

"When I come back, I better get an answer and I better not hear any sirens," he said and started walking up the stairs.

I shook my head and slumped in the chair.

Lacey was my only hope. Well, it could've been anyone, but I could only remember her phone number.

All she needed to do was to get the f*cking contract my foster parents had signed. Then she would've taken it to the cops, and they could've come arrest this f*cker in the quietest way possible.

But Morgan intervened.

If she hadn't told me to get out of her room, I wouldn't have shown up home and wouldn't have gotten sold off.

This isn't her fault. You're just trying to blame her for what she said.

I sighed at my conscience.

Morgan bothered the sh*t out of me, but I admit I liked her a lot.

Even if she thought I was a failure.

Winnie came back, munching on a sandwich, and gave me a look. "Who did you call?"

I really needed to find a f*cking way out of here.

CHAPTER TWENTY-FOUR
Team Up with His Ex to Find Him

MORGAN COLLINS

I opened the door to Dad's office with Lacey in tow.

"Dad, I know what happened to Mas—"

"Morgan," he spoke through gritted teeth. His eyes shot daggers at me as he set down a stack of papers. "I know you aren't trying to get involved in Mason's case."

"He was sold," I blurted out before he could stop me.

My dad looked at me expectantly and Lacey continued, "He told me there was a contract in his foster parent's house. He told me to find it and to give it to you."

My dad sighed and stood up, taking a few steps closer to us. "Girls . . . even if that was true, we couldn't search their house until we get a warrant, and I strongly urge you not to go and find it yourself."

I looked at Lacey and nodded. "Okay, Dad, that's cool."

He looked surprised as if me agreeing with him was a first.

He nodded at us before ushering us towards the door.

"We can't just leave him in there until the cops get the warrant." Lacey shook her head as she fiddled with her car keys.

"We're not. We're going to find that contract."

* * *

I am f*cking hungry. What day is it? Friday? Saturday?

"What day is it?" I called out to the woman who was in charge of watching me.

She was around my age, maybe a few years older. Curly blonde hair framed her face and her brown eyes stood out against her porcelain skin.

She was okay, not ugly but certainly not pretty. She looked a lot like Winnie, which is probably why I couldn't stomach the thought of her.

I shook the thoughts away.

"Why would I tell you?"

"Fine then. Be a b*tch." I shrugged and looked down at my tied hands. I needed something sharp.

"Maybe you can give me something in return, you know," she murmured suggestively as she made her way towards me.

I winced. "I have no teeth, and I'm covered in my own blood," I said in a deadpan manner.

She sighed as if she had just noticed and took a peek at the door. She bit her lip before untying me from my chair.

She made sure to keep my hands tied and held a sharp knife to my back. "Walk," she ordered.

"Alright," I murmured.

"My name's Pamela." She smiled and led me towards a bathroom.

As if I actually gave a f*ck what her name was.

"Okay. Strip and don't try anything funny," Pamela ordered and pointed the knife at me.

I raised a brow. "Wow, not even two hours of knowing each other and you're already asking me to get naked."

She didn't look amused.

I sighed.

"I can't take off my shirt," I pointed out and gestured at my tied hands.

Pamela hesitated but cut off the rope before pointing the knife again at me as if to reassure she had no problem with stabbing me.

Dumb b*tch.

I caught her wrist and twisted it until she let go of the knife.

"Oww," she shrieked and I pulled her wrist, making her face-plant onto the floor.

She hissed as I circled her. I tied her hands with the little rope left. "You smell like ass," she said.

"Yeah, tough sh*t," I mumbled before picking myself up. I needed to get out of here before Winnie found out I had beaten up his daughter.

I made a sharp turn and ran down the stairs, cussing when I felt my left leg burn.

"F*ck me," I growled but didn't stop to check it.

I threw the door open and cursed. "F*ck!" I came face to face with Winnie. "What are the f*cking odds?"

"Going somewhere?" He eyed me and set down what seemed to be his groceries on the floor.

I shrugged. "I was just going to take a walk, so if you'll excuse me."

I stepped to the side, but he mimicked my move, raising an eyebrow at me.

"Can't blame a guy for trying." I smirked before using all my force to punch him.

He stumbled back and shouted out a name, but I didn't stop to see who the f*ck it was.

I f*cking ran as fast as I could, ignoring the ache that sprouted in my leg.

Morgan.

126

As cliché and dumb as it sounded, she was the only person keeping me alive. She was a f*cking dumbass, and I couldn't bear her, but I liked her. I wanted to see her.

I tripped and bit my tongue to hold the cry bubbling at my throat. I looked towards my leg and shook my head once I saw my jeans soaked in blood.

"F*ck," I murmured.

I was sure Winnie had beaten the f*ck out of me, but I hadn't actually felt much of it due to adrenaline.

I pulled my jeans up and sighed once I saw the state my leg was in.

The part above my knee was a deep purple. I don't think anything was broken, but it hurt like—

My ears perked up at the cock of a gun, and I closed my eyes slowly.

"Your leg's a little f*cked up." It wasn't Winnie.

He circled around me and kicked my leg full force, kneeling beside me.

I couldn't stop the groan that passed my lips as I held onto my leg desperately.

"Your face is very f*cked up, and you don't hear me saying sh*t." The man grit his teeth and pointed his gun at my head, clicking his tongue. "I don't think you want to insult a man with a gun."

Morgan's face popped into my head.

She was beautiful. Her green eyes, long brown hair, and her f*cking obsession to bother the sh*t out of me were all beautiful. I couldn't leave her.

I had to survive for her.

"Fine, I—" I was cut off by the ringing in my ears.

It had taken me a while to realize that the man had shot the gun and a bit more to make me feel the pain in my leg.

"So you won't run again," he reassured and I started to see black spots in the corner of my eyes.

Before I could remark, everything went black.

CHAPTER TWENTY-FIVE
Save Him

MORGAN COLLINS

Lacey hissed as she peeked past the door of Robert and Diana's room. "Hurry the f*ck up!"

"I'm trying," I spat back at her as I nervously scattered through the drawers.

"You f*cking slow ass piece of sh*t," Lacey grumbled as she closed the door slowly. "Let me look."

"No, b*tch, we agreed you would watch and I would l—"

She pushed me aside and pulled out a piece of paper before giving me a look. "Seriously?" Lacey gave me a deadpan face as she held up the paper. "It was right here."

I growled and stood up. "Shut the f*ck up. Let's get out of here before—"

We both froze at the sound of a door slamming shut.

"I'm just saying, hentai isn't the type of porn I'd want . . ."

Lacey looked at me wide-eyed as the voices got louder. I quickly pointed under the bed. Both of us dove under it, occasionally shoving each other, before Robert and Diana came in.

"Oh, baby!" Diana moaned as they both landed on the bed.

I turned to look at Lacey in horror as the bed started to creak. *My f*cking sh*t luck.*

MASON HUNTER

I opened my eyes groggily and groaned at the pain blossoming in my thigh. How long did I sleep?

"I told you to catch him, not to f*cking kill him," Winnie growled as his wife placed his soup in front of him.

I shifted my leg, almost rolling my eyes when I felt rope.

These dumb f*cks really decided to tie my injured leg to the table as if I had so much of a possibility of running away.

"He was getting on my nerves, Dad," the other guy mumbled, taking a spoonful of his soup.

"Eat, honey," Winnie's wife encouraged as she gestured towards my bowl. "You need the energy."

I sympathized with the woman. Living with these crackheads must be driving her crazy.

I took a spoon, not caring what it contained at this point, and poured the soup in my mouth.

"I say we just kill him," Pamela hissed. The purple bruise on her forehead had gotten much worse.

I nodded. "Literally anything would be better than hearing you sh*t-for-brains argue."

"Why you little—" Winnie's son started but was cut off by Winnie.

"Don't kill my investment, boy." Winnie threw a harsh kick to my leg.

I bit my tongue and closed my eyes.

I really want to die.

"F*ck. You're a f*cking grown ass man. You're really going to let your dad talk to you like that?" I mocked, earning another kick.

A groan escaped my lips this time.

"Trina!" Winnie exclaimed and a petite blonde girl rushed from the kitchen.

She looked younger than me, maybe about fifteen. Her clothes were ragged, and she looked beat down both physically and emotionally.

"Clean up Mason's blood." He flicked his wrist dismissively, and Trina almost jumped at the small action.

"Anyways—did you hear that?"

"Hear what?" Pamela asked.

"I heard something, Billy. Go check the house."

"Will do, Pops!"

I drowned out their conversation as I watched Trina fall to her knees and scrub vigorously at the wooden floor.

"Hey," I mumbled softly. "How long have you been here?"

Trina's bottom lip quivered and she quickly wiped a traitorous tear from her cheek.

"I don't know," she whispered. "It feels like I've been here for an eternity."

I gulped at her words, finally coming to the realization that I might be here forever too. What if no one found me? What if I never saw Morgan again?

"I'm going to get you out of here, Trina," I promised even though I had no f*cking idea how I was going to do it now that I was crippled.

She looked at me, and I watched as a spark of hope lit up in her green eyes.

"Trina," Winnie growled. "No talking. Don't make me f*cking beat you."

"Hey, f*ck off, assmuncher!" I spat back. I didn't know why I was willing to take the beating for her. I didn't even know her. Winnie stood up quickly and pushed me back. I winced as the rope pulled on my leg.

"I'm so f*cking sick of you and your smart mouth," he hissed as he took a pistol from his back pocket and pointed it to my head.

I chuckled and shook my head. "You think I'm afraid to die?"

This only seemed to anger him more. "What do I have to do to get a reaction from you?"

"Hey!"

Winnie and I both turned our heads to the source of the sound, and I turned white as I saw Morgan being held by Billy.

"Found her right outside," Billy admitted proudly. "Isn't she a doll?"

"Who the f*ck is she?" Pamela grimaced.

"I-I," Morgan stammered as she glanced at me in horror. "I'm Morgan Collins?"

I had to bite my tongue to not scream at her.

*What is she doing here? Why the f*ck did she come alone?*

Winnie looked at her and then back at me, and I could practically see the gears turning in his head.

She's what he needs to get a reaction from me.

A sick smile made its way onto his face. "Bring her over here."

Billy did as he was asked and shoved Morgan forwards.

"Do you know her, Mason?" Winnie asked, turning his gun over to her.

"No," I mumbled.

"She's a really pretty girl," he suggested. "She will make a great deal, don't ya think?"

I looked over at Morgan, who looked oddly calm for this situation, and back at Winnie.

"Okay, what the f*ck do you want my advice for?" I shrugged, hoping Morgan would play along. The last thing I wanted was for her to die because of me.

Winnie cocked his gun and pointed it back at me. "Well, with a pretty face like hers, I don't think I need you anymore."

I knew he was bluffing. He wanted to get a reaction from me, but Morgan didn't seem to catch on.

"Please no!" Morgan's eyes widened in fear.

She had always been such a f*cking dumbass.

Winnie smirked. "I think she knows you, Mason."

Before any of us could react, Morgan slapped the gun out of his hand and she screamed out a string of words.

Almost instantly, the dining room was filled with cops, all pointing their guns at Winnie.

"Taylor Hoffman, you're arrested for kidnapping, drug possession, and human trafficking," a man said. "Put your hands where I can see them."

Morgan rushed to my side and made a face when she saw the state I was in. "Teeth are overrated anyways."

"Why the f*ck did you risk your life like that?" I growled as she untied the rope from my leg.

"I mean, a whole SWAT team couldn't just rush in while he was pointing a gun at your head."

"You're a f*cking idiot. I can't believe I like you." I shook my head and she froze.

"Wait, you like me?"

"We will shoot," a man announced. "Put your hands up."

From the corner of my eye, I saw Billy pick up the gun, and before I could even sit up, he pulled the trigger.

EPILOGUE

MORGAN COLLINS

You know that angsty teen in your school? The boy with tattoos? The one started sh*t for absolutely no reason? You know, the bad boy? Every school had one. You either knew him, had an unpleasant interaction with him, or heard about him at least once.

Whichever it was, you probably wanted nothing to do with him.

And you're probably right, you should stay the F*CK away from him.

"Seventeen, female, shot on the right side of her body, no signs of organ failure."

"Is she alright?"

I heard Mason exclaim from the other gurney in the ambulance. My vision was starting to fail me, but I could barely see the other paramedic blocking him.

"She's losing a lot of blood, Adam," the paramedic screamed as she packed a few more pads on the wound.

"Is there an exit wound?" Adam replied and roughly turned around, leaving Mason for a bit.

"I don't know! This is my first day!"

Of course, leave it to my bad luck to choose my f*cking paramedic.

"Get him the f*ck away from me. I don't want this pussy ass rookie touching me." That's what I tried to say, but the only thing you could fully understand was "F*ck . . . Pussy . . . Touching me."

"What the f*ck is happening? Is she okay?"

"Sir, please stay in your gurney. Everything will be fine."

"Traumatic pneumothorax," Adam whispered and my eyelids started to flutter suddenly. "The bullet punctured the lung! We need a chest tube!"

My eyes widened as he pulled out a thick ass tube, and I tried to shake my head.

*Oh no, this f*cking newbie is going to kill me.*

My eyes started to flutter, and before I knew it, I saw pitch black.

I opened my eyes again, expecting to see the paramedics and Mason, but instead caught sight of a dark figure lingering in a corner.

"Morgan Collins?" it spoke.

"Yeah?" I responded lowly as I took a look at my surroundings. The room was mostly white, and the only things in it were me and the figure that started making its way towards me.

He peeled off his hood, revealing a lanky tall boy with piercing blue eyes.

"I'm Death," he introduced as he scribbled on his clipboard. "It's your time."

What the f*ck was this? 27 days?

"Um," I stammered. "What about Mason?"

"Honey, do you know the number of Masons in the world? You have to be a bit more specific."

"Mason Hunter," I suggested and received a brow raise from him.

"Alessandro Warren," I said again.

He sighed and raved his clipboard one more time. "Yeah, he's not coming in today. Are we done? Can we leave now? I kinda have a tight schedule."

I scoffed. "Okay, you don't have to be such a f*cking dick."

He took my arm and led me towards a door. "At least I didn't run into a gun fight."

I looked at him dryly. He got me there.

"Can I at least say bye to my family?"

Death scoffed and halted in his steps. "What does this look like to you? A crappy teen book? You think I'm going to give you a chance to go see your sh*tty ass boyfriend and your family? This is real life, Morgan Collins. You're dead. There's no turning back."

"Look, you f*cking skeleton ass motherf*cker. I could use a bit of f*cking support here instead of you sh*tting on me."

"If you don't shut up, I'm sending you straight to hell."

My lips sealed shut and I looked back, noticing a vivid image of Mason crying over my now dead body.

"Ew, what the f*ck. I look like sh*t—"

"F*ck, Morgan Collins. I'm sending you back, you annoying piece of sh*t mortal," Death growled, suddenly turning around.

"Wha—" Death clicked his fingers, and I slowly opened my eyes, noticing Mason above me.

"She's breathing!" Adam exclaimed, flabbergasted by the whole thing. "Huh, I must be pretty good."

Mason looked at me, his golden orbs staring into my soul.

"You look like a f*cking idiot without teeth," I murmured in a strained voice.

"You look like a f*cking idiot in general," he shot back as his thumb trailed down my cheek. "You scared the living f*ck out of me. You're so f*cking stup—"

"I won't do it again. I promise," I cut him off. "We're going to be okay."

136

I believed it, even at this moment with a f*cking tube shoved into my body, with a very attractive toothless man, and with a very annoyed ass Death. I believed everything was going to be okay.

As long as I had this f*cking dumbass by my side.

"I know this is probably the worst time possible, but do you want to go out to eat, like on a date? I'll show up and you can pay for me. That's pretty much a deal. I don't know why you would ever reje—"

"I'd love to," he smiled and grabbed my hand forcefully. "Just don't die."

I laughed and then groaned once I felt a sharp pain on my left side.

"No promises," I mumbled as I pulled him in for a kiss.

"Adam, what the f*ck is happening?"

"I don't know, Jerry. Just let it be."

Do you like YA stories?
Here are samples of other stories
you might enjoy!

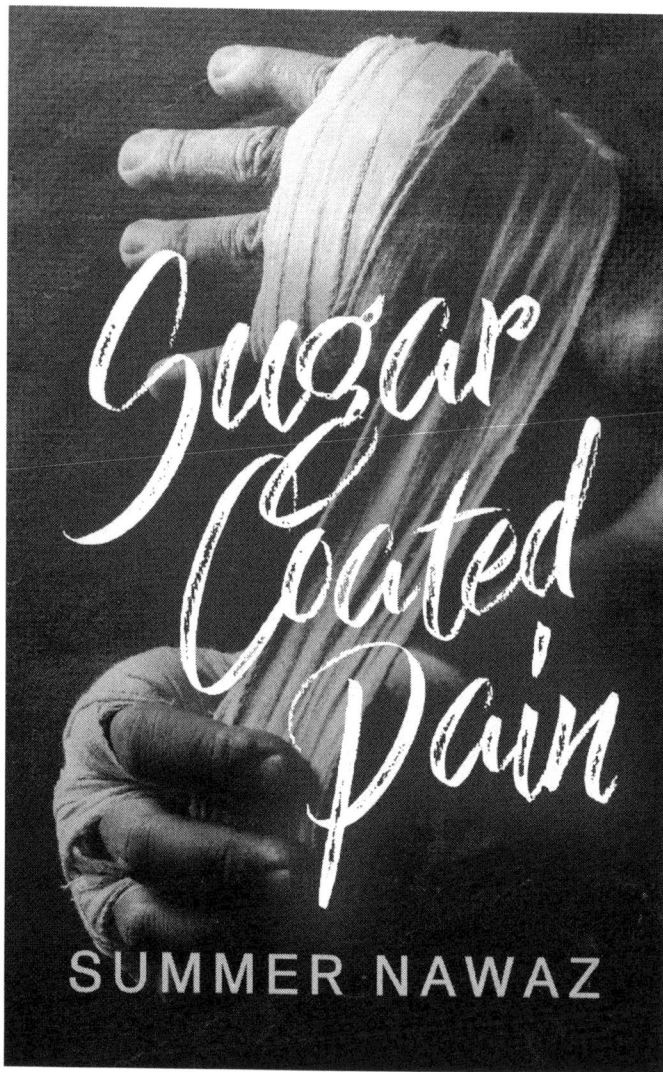

Sugar Coated Pain

SUMMER NAWAZ

CHAPTER ONE

The feel of the hardcover in her hands and the smell of new books that greeted her every time she picked them up comforted Noelle Simon as she continued her work. She was currently fixing up the horror or thriller section of the store she helped run, replacing the sold out books with copies she picked up from the inventory earlier. Once she was satisfied with how a shelf looked, she moved on to the next one.

While she normally enjoyed doing this, her sister talking her ear off made it difficult for Noelle to work peacefully.

"Come on, Elle," her twenty-four-year-old sister, Beverly, whined to her left. "He just wants to take us out. You like Aiden. Why're you being so difficult?"

"Because I don't wanna be a third wheel," Noelle replied, putting up copies of Bram Stoker novels as she shot her blonde sister a pointed look. "I do like Aiden, but you two end up in your own little world. I don't wanna be sitting there all awkward and shit."

Beverly huffed, glossy lips forming a pout. "I promise we'll try to hold back on that," she insisted, shuffling forward as Noelle moved further down the aisle. "Andrea loves going out with us, and it's about time you come too. We're not that bad, I swear," she added with a laugh.

What Beverly said was true; Noelle liked Aiden. She had no reason not to. Knowing there was something special about him for her sister the day, almost a year ago, that Beverly called her up to gush about the absolutely divine—Beverly's exact words—instructor who worked at the new gym she went to. They met last summer, right after Beverly graduated from college and was getting ready to fully run Simon's Stories on her own. It was a miracle given that Beverly took a year off after high school to do some traveling. She was convinced she didn't want to go back to college until she finally gave in on her own accord. Aiden had been a lender of support when she took over the business, which sometimes overwhelmed Beverly, and Noelle was too busy finishing up her own last year of college to be of much help. He was a good guy.

Not only did he treat Beverly well but Aiden also had a soft spot to their seventeen-year-old sister Andrea, bringing her along to nice outings as well. Noelle only met Aiden a handful of times despite him being with Beverly for the past year, but that was because Noelle was living in New Jersey for college. Now that she was back in the city and having just graduated a few weeks ago, Aiden wanted to take them out for dinner. While that wasn't strange and Noelle adored Aiden, she genuinely didn't want to be a third wheel.

When Beverly wanted something, she would insist and persuade until she would get it. Noelle could already feel her fight leaving her. She knew she was a bit of a pushover, especially when it came to her sisters, but Noelle didn't really care about that unless she absolutely had to stand her ground on something. Unfortunately, this didn't qualify.

"Why do we have to go to Brooklyn though?" she finally complained.

A smile began spreading on Beverly's lips, knowing she had talked her sister into dinner. "Because one of Aiden's friends opened up a restaurant there, and he hasn't tried it out yet." She smiled excitedly. "We'll get free dessert!"

Noelle shot her a dry smile, raising an eyebrow as she pushed the almost empty cart with her hip. "But dinner isn't free?" She clicked her tongue teasingly. "Then what's the point?"

"It is for us. It's Aiden's treat." Beverly laughed, shaking her head and walking past Noelle to go to the front of the store. "He'll pick us up at home at seven-thirty!"

*   *   *

Despite her initial hesitance, Noelle would be lying if she said she wasn't enjoying her time. It was nearing 9 PM, and she's been seated in the restaurant for about an hour and a half, finding it difficult to swallow a sip of her wine as she laughed at yet another joke Aiden made. They were almost finished eating, and Noelle was savoring every taste of her Penne alla Vodka.

They were in an adorable and quaint Italian restaurant with sleek floors and dark walls that went nicely with the red chairs and white tables. The soft glow of the individual lamps hanging from the ceilings over each table provided a calming ambiance. The restaurant was right by the East River, and Aiden had gotten them a table on the upstairs patio that had fairy lights strung above their heads. The breeze was gentle against her skin, and the view of the Brooklyn Bridge kept demanding Noelle's attention.

"How much did you miss the city?" Aiden asked Noelle once they calmed down from their laughter, leaning back in his chair. "Or have you become a Jersey girl?".

Noelle snorted, picking up her almost empty glass of wine once more. "I'm always gonna be a city girl," she confirmed as Beverly smirked, "and I'm proud of it."

Aiden grinned, dimples in full view as he opened his mouth to say something, only to be cut off by the sound of his phone ringing. "Sorry." He shot Beverly and Noelle apologetic smiles as he answered the call, looking out over the railing they were sitting next to, towards the river.

"Hey, what's up?" The girls took this time to finish their food but didn't miss the sudden change of Aiden's tone as he practically hissed into the phone, "What?"

Noelle's eyes widened slightly at the harshness in Aiden's voice, drastically different than the usual excited, pleasant lilt his tone held whenever she talked to him. She glanced at Beverly, who didn't at all look fazed by his demeanor and instead had her eyebrows lowered in concern.

Am I missing something? Noelle thought.

"He's not scheduled for toni—" Aiden stopped, face contorted into a scowl as he listened to whoever was on the other end, still looking out towards the water. Noelle watched as Aiden clenched his jaw, his free hand running through his short curly hair, then he kept his fingers entangled at the back of his head. "Max, he's booked for the next two nights. He had tonight off for a goddamn reason."

Whatever Aiden was talking about sounded like some kind of work scheduling conflict to Noelle's ears. She knew Aiden was a fitness instructor at a gym in Manhattan, but the way he was speaking—the hard edge in his voice and severe frustration on his face—made whatever he was talking about sound like a really big deal. When she looked at Beverly, Noelle saw realization flitter across her sister's face, but there was still worry etched onto her features.

Aiden's hazel eyes glanced over the two girls quickly. "I can't. I'm in the middle of dinner," he said into the phone before letting out a sigh and rubbing his hand down his face. He looked both riled up and defeated at the same time. "Fuck. Okay, alright. I'll be there in ten."

Noelle's eyebrows shot up at that. *Is dinner over already?*

"I'm sorry to have to do this, girls," Aiden apologized, his expression softening as he looked at them with a sheepish smile while pocketing his phone and taking out his wallet. "I have to get to Astros. It's Car," he said as his gaze met Beverly's.

Beverly's lips parted, evidently understanding what Aiden was talking about as he raised his hand for the waiter and gestured for the check while Noelle sat there, staring at the two of them in confusion. *What the hell is Astros and who is Car?*

"Um, what's going on?" she questioned, letting her bewilderment be known as she shook her head slightly and persistently.

The check arrived promptly, and Aiden didn't even bother looking at it as he put his credit card in and gave the little black folder back to the waiter. Noelle stared at her sister with a questioning raise of her eyebrows because, apparently, she knew exactly what was going on. "Oh, um . . . it's just—"

"She'll see when we get there, Bev," Aiden cut her off, looking around impatiently for the waiter to return with his card. The muscle in his jaw was jumping, agitation practically radiating off of him. He looked so frantic, a complete deviation from his normal easy-going personality Noelle was used to.

Noelle watched as Beverly shot a wide-eyed look at the man. "Are you joking?" she demanded, her own tone taking a hard edge to it. Noelle blinked, not expecting her sister to suddenly get so disconcerted. Beverly leaned closer to Aiden. "Noelle isn't going there," she said, dropping her tone.

Aiden looked exasperated even as the waiter returned to give back the folder. Aiden quickly took out his card and shoved it back in his wallet. "I have to get there ASAP, Bev. I'm not about to let either of you take the subway or Uber back home, okay? We don't have a choice, doll," he said to Beverly as he signed the receipt.

Okay. What the hell is going on? Noelle thought.

Aiden quickly stood up from his chair, looking like he couldn't get out of here fast enough. Beverly's jaw was clenched tightly, and she looked irritated as soon as Aiden said that Noelle would be coming with them. Meanwhile, the brunette slowly rose from her seat, trying to catch her sister's eye as she wondered why Beverly didn't want her going to this "Astro" place.

Noelle followed in silent bewilderment, frowning at the backs of Beverly and Aiden as they had an intense yet whispered conversation right in front of her while making their way out of the building. She was growing irritated at their lack of communication towards her, leaving her in the dark as they stepped out onto the sidewalk and approached Aiden's car. From the bits and pieces Noelle could gather, Beverly was still arguing that she didn't want Noelle to go to Astros, and Aiden was apologizing that there was no other way.

Beverly didn't bother hiding her distaste in the situation as they got in the car. "I don't like this." She heard her sister mutter as she slid in the back.

Don't like what? Noelle wanted to scream, watching Aiden let out a sigh as he buckled his seatbelt. "I know, doll. I'm sorry, but I have to go for Car."

Noelle clenched her jaw. She didn't like being in the dark. *Who the hell is Car?*

If you enjoyed this sample, look for
Sugarcoated Pain
on Amazon.

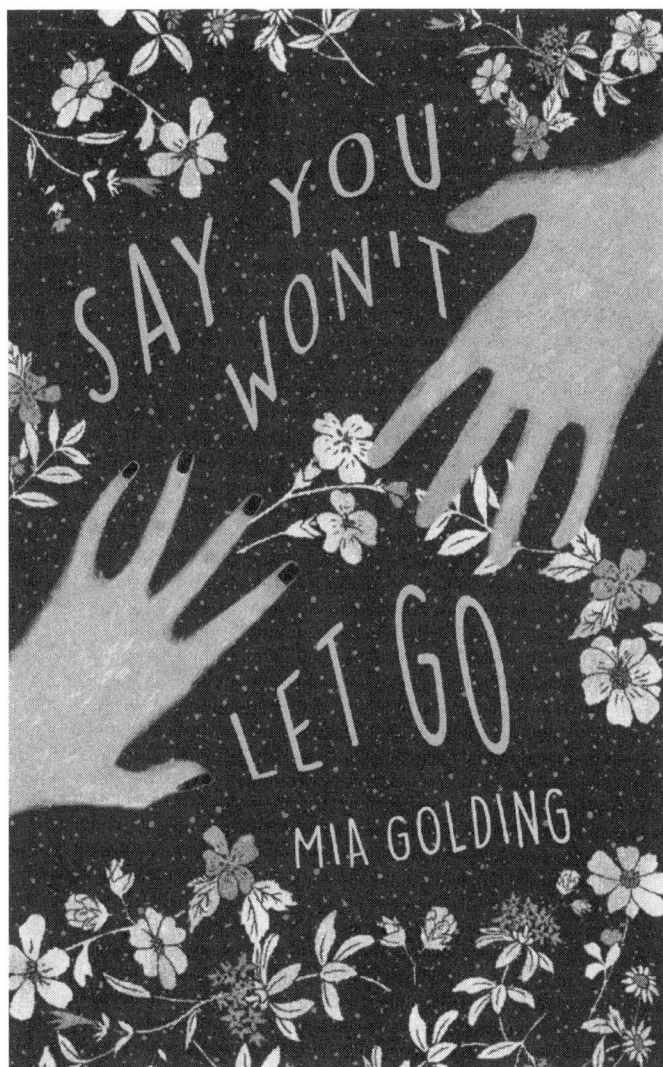

SAY YOU WON'T

LET GO

MIA GOLDING

CHAPTER ONE

The worst part about losing someone is losing them when you least expect it. It's not every day you have your parents break the news to you that your best friend has committed suicide. It's one of those days where I just have that gut feeling that something is bound to go wrong—and trust me, I've had more than one of those days—but never in my life could I have imagined something going this wrong.

The memory of hearing of my best friend's death is as fresh in my mind as ink on a sheet of paper. The days after hearing of her death are a blur of tears and locking myself in my room all day, convincing myself that this is all just some cruel joke. I soon learned this to be the first stage of grieving—denial. I'm not ready to move on, but I know I have to try because even if she isn't here to live her life with me, I know that she will want me to live mine for the both of us. Even if I'm still angry and confused about why hers ended.

*   *   *

I sit in my car and stare up at my high school. The lawn is littered with teens conversing about what they did over break, going on as if absolutely nothing has changed when it feels like my whole world has changed. Taking a deep breath, I grab my things before opening the car door and stepping out. Putting my head down, I try to walk briskly into the building without having to run into anyone.

"Alexa!" *Just my luck.*

"Paige, hi." I force some enthusiasm into my voice, but it just ends up falling flat. "I heard what happened, and the girls and I just wanted to say sorry for your loss. If you ever need anything, I will be happy to help," she says with what I can obviously tell is fake sincerity. I look at her and the rest of the girls sitting at a table a few feet away.

"Thanks for your concern, Paige," I say, forcing down any hint of anger. "But I'm fine." I abruptly turn around and walk away before she can get a chance to reply.

Walking through the crowded hallway, I glance at the place where my best friend's locker used to be. The place where I would meet with her every day to complain about how awful our mornings were as we headed to our first class together. The place I will no longer be going to every morning. I trudge through the halls with memories surging my mind as I try hard not to break down right here and now. It's hard enough waking up this morning and driving past her house on my way here, but this . . . this just adds salt to the wound. The shrill ringing of the bell breaks me out of my trance, and I hurry to my locker before heading off to my first class of the day.

I can't seem to focus as Ms. Anderson promptly starts the lesson. I can't stop hearing her voice at the back of my head or picturing her next to me, not paying attention to the lesson at all as she makes snarky comments about how awful Ms. Anderson's outfit choice is that day.

"Alexa? Ms. Parker, are you with us?" The sound of Ms. Anderson's saccharine voice interrupts any further thoughts, and I try to clear my head.

"Yes. Sorry," I say quickly. She gives me a sympathetic look before continuing with the lesson, a lump forming in my throat. Time seems to be moving agonizingly slow as my next few classes go by; it doesn't help that every few minutes, I am approached by people saying how sorry they are for my loss and how she was such an amazing person. Half of them don't even know her. It infuriates me that these people didn't give her a second thought when she was alive, but now that she's dead, she suddenly matters to them.

When lunch finally comes around, I sit at a table towards the back. I'm relieved to get a break and a chance to sort my thoughts. My break is short-lived as I'm joined by company.

"Hi, Alexa. How are you?" Alison greets timidly as she and Madison sit down with their lunch trays. Alison and Madison are twins and probably the sweetest girls you will ever meet, but right now, I just wish they will get up and leave. I'm tired of people coming up to me with their pity and condolences, which only reminds me more of my loss.

"I'm fine," I reply half-heartedly, not having it in me to ask them to leave. "What brings you guys here?"

"Can't we have lunch with our captain?" Madison says with that bright smile that can light up any room.

"We just want to check on you, and the team wants to know if you'll be at cheer practice today." *Right. There's practice.*

"Yeah, totally." I flash them a smile. I can't let them see my weakness, and if moving on means that I have to resume the role of the girl I was before that day, then so be it. As lunch progresses and they make no move to leave, I struggle to stay focused. Everything reminds me of her.

The table near the center of the room used to be our table. The table we would sit at every day and talk about boys while also discussing our future. She would always talk about how we would attend the same college and become roommates and then rent an apartment together in a different city after graduation. It all just keeps leading me back to the question of 'why?'. I can feel my eyes start to blur with tears, and I stand up suddenly. The twins look up at me with concern-filled eyes.

"I-I'm going to go. I just remembered I have to go to the library and check out a book for my next class," I say while grabbing my things.

"Oh okay. I guess we'll see you at practice?" Alison asks.

"I'll be there," I promise her.

I emerge from the cafeteria and make my way to the bathroom with my eyes locked on the ground so no one can see the tears ready to fall.

"Sorry," I say after accidentally bumping into someone, not even bothering to look at them as I start to sprint to the bathroom in my frantic state. After making sure it's empty, I slide against the wall and do the one thing I promised myself I wouldn't do today— I cry. The tears pour out like a waterfall, the confusion and anger and pain with them. I cry until my vision is blurry and my eyes are red. I cry until I know that I can't be in here any longer because someone is bound to walk in, and I'm not sure I can handle confrontation in this state. It's been a month since she's been gone, and instead of things getting easier with time, everything seems to be getting harder. I wish that I can just go back in time and stop any of this from happening.

It's taking me some time to compose myself. I missed the remainder of my classes for the day, and I can't even bring myself to care. I end up leaving cheer practice early at the suggestion of the team. I can't focus on the routine, and I was messing everything up. Pushing through the double doors of the gym, I let out a frustrated sigh as I lean against the wall and pinch the bridge of my nose. I eventually head to the school's parking lot, which is mostly empty with the exception of a few cars.

"Alexa?" I hear my name being called and I go rigid. *Why can't I be left alone?*

"Hey, Matt." I turn to look at him and his friends surrounding his truck with sweat and dirt running down their faces. Matt Carpenter is the quarterback of our school's football team. I don't really recall having any real interactions with him other than at football games.

"It's been awhile since I've seen you," he says.

"I have a lot going on at the moment." I unlock my car door, not caring to continue this conversation after the crap day I've had.

"Wait," he says as I'm about to make my escape. I look at him expectantly, feeling annoyed that I'm being delayed from leaving.

"I'm sorry but I need to go." I shut my car door and leave, not allowing myself to feel bad for how harsh that probably sounded. When I finally enter my house, I'm greeted by the smell of my mother's cooking.

Before, I would be rushing into the kitchen, anxious to get a bite of whatever was on the stove. Now, I barely have an appetite.

"How was school?" she inquires with a smile as I throw my keys down on to the table.

"It was okay." Sighing, I watch as she dumps some pasta into the pot of boiling water.

"You know you can talk to me, Alexa. What happened isn't something you can easily recover from," she starts with a soft gaze in her eyes as she looks at me. "I know you both were close but—" I clench my hands into fists at her words.

We weren't *just* close; she was all I had. She's the only person that understood me, and now, she's gone. No explanation, no warning, and no apology.

"Mom, I know you're trying to help me and I appreciate it; I really do, but I just need time and space. She's my best friend and I don't want to think about the fact that she's gone." She looks taken aback by my words but she nods anyway.

"Okay. Well, I'm here if you need anything. I just want you to know that you're not alone," she replies with a sad smile, and I give her a quick hug before heading upstairs to my room. I lock the door and collapse on to my bed as I stare up at the ceiling. I grab my journal from the nightstand and open it up to a clean page but I freeze as a picture falls out.

It's of her and I at a party. We were holding red solo cups—which were filled with ginger ale—and smiling like there was no tomorrow.

"I can't believe you did that!" I exclaim as we both stumble into my room, hunched over in fits of laughter. "The look on her face was priceless!"

"It was definitely an accident," Cam says with a smirk.

"I think Paige knows you spilling that drink on her wasn't an accident."

I shut the journal and hold it tightly to my chest. It isn't fair. It isn't fair that Cam is gone, and I'm expected to just move on. How can I when most of my happiest memories are with her? How can I when all I can think about is her day in and day out? The tears fall down my cheeks for what feels like the thousandth time today. I curl into a ball with the picture clenched against my chest. I don't know how long I stayed like that, but before I know it, I'm asleep.

If you enjoyed this sample, look for
Say You Won't Let Go
on Amazon.

ALI MERCI

through
your eyes

01.
Asa

Asa's grandpa had once told him that his rash nature and tendency to act on impulse would get him in trouble one day.

It got Asa in trouble, all right. More than just once.

And it seemed like today was just another one of those days.

It wasn't Asa's fault. Not really. He just didn't like it when Hunter Donoghue spoke. Or moved. Or breathed for that matter.

"Take that, *pinche pendejo!*" Asa's fist landed on Hunter's jaw with a sickening crack, and the linebacker stumbled several feet backwards, thrown off-balance. He was still standing and not sprawled out on the ground, though. Not what Asa would've preferred.

Hunter's eyes flashed dangerously and, within the short space of two breaths, he lunged forward in a half-bent posture, ramming his head into Asa's stomach.

Asa groaned, all air knocked out of his lungs for what felt like an eternity. Both of them stumbled to the ground, Asa's back hitting the tiled hallway floors of Reichenbach High with Hunter's heavy body pinning him down.

Without a moment's hesitation, Asa shoved Hunter's body off of him, muttering a string of colourful words in the process.

"You absolute piece of garbage." Asa wheezed, his breaths coming in gasps. He clutched his abdomen where Hunter's head had collided.

"Oh, grow the hell up," Hunter sneered, his lips curling back over his teeth in a nasty snarl. "Trying to be the hero isn't going to get you anywhere."

"But bullying will?"

In answer, Hunter lunged at him again, but this time Asa had prepared himself. He used one of his feet to hook itself behind Hunter's shins, sending him to the ground.

Hunter hit the ground with a strangled yell but it was soon cut off when Asa pounced on him, driving a fist into his gut in retaliation for head-butting him earlier.

"Dude, what's your problem?!" Hunter grabbed a fistful of Asa's collar and struck him with a closed fist across his face.

Asa's head whipped to the side, but he only laughed in response to the question. "You," he spat. "People like you are my problem. What the hell is it to you how much someone eats?"

Hunter struggled, but he eventually managed to throw an aggressive Asa off him, quickly moving back a few steps as the latter did the same.

Both of the boys kept their eyes fixed on each other, their well-muscled frames tensed in anticipation of another round of punches, kicks and blows.

"She piles her plate every goddamn day with food enough to feed an army!" Hunter rolled his shoulders back, a gleam in his eyes as he watched Asa with a smirk. "I was only asking her to leave some for the rest of us." He shrugged, oozing with nonchalance and arrogance. "She could do with shedding off the extra weight. I mean, look at her."

Asa's eyes tore away from cautiously watching Hunter and landed on the girl standing a few feet away from them, curled up by the corner of the wall and the lockers, scared and terrified. His gut clenched at the sight, only adding more fuel to his hatred for the boy standing in front of him.

It had been right after English period, just as the lunch bell rang, when Asa had heard Hunter's mocking voice from the other end of the hallway He'd known in his bones by then that the prick was up to no good.

He'd arrived just in time to hear Hunter's less than pleasant words to the girl, the kind that echoed in someone's mind for days, corrupting it so that, later, it would shape the way they saw themselves.

The familiarity of it all had hit Asa somewhere deep in the chest.

And then came the blinding rage, and suddenly, fists were flown and profanities were spewed out from each other's mouths. It was a wonder nobody heard them and a crowd didn't congregate around the two boys yet.

Asa looked back at Hunter's unapologetic eyes. "She looks fine to me," he said. "More human than you, anyway."

Hunter looked prepared to lunge at him again, but a shrill voice—that often reminded Asa of the whistle of the Hogwarts Express—cut through the tense air.

"What's going on here?" asked the screeching voice.

He hated *that* voice.

The boys shook off their predatory stance, lowering their fists and unclenching their palms. Mrs. Cromwell, their disciplinary head, was someone on the list of school authorities one simply did not mess with.

"Still having trouble keeping your fists to yourself, San Román?" Cromwell's beady, soulless eyes looked down from her nose at Asa as she took in the bruises and the cuts on him.

"Me? You're blaming *just* me? You don't even know what he did—" But Asa's retort was cut short by that same nails-on-walls voice.

"Mr. San Román," she curled her lips when she said his name, "I think it's pretty well-known how you can be biased towards anything that involves Mr. Donoghue, so pardon me if I don't take your account of what happened seriously."

Asa snorted. "And what? You think the animosity is one-sided? How is his version of events going to be any more honest?"

"Well, I guess you're just going to have to live with that, Mr. San—"

"Oh, for god's sake!" He stood to his full height and scowled at Mrs. Cromwell. "It's *Asa*. San Román is the family name. I get that you seem to like using that name, but would you mind?"

Mrs. Cromwell's cheeks coloured, her hands shaking by her sides, as if she wanted to smack Asa's head

"Watch it, young man. I do not appreciate being told what to do by the apes that come to this school."

Asa raised a brow. "Does that include you too, Ma'am? I mean, you *do* attend this school, too." From his peripheral view, Asa could see Hunter's shoulders shake with silent laughter as he tried to suppress it.

"Detention!" she boomed, her voice echoing throughout the deserted hallway. "For the rest of the week."

Asa's scowl deepened. He opened his mouth, ready to tell the stupid disciplinarian what had happened, when his eye caught the girl's movements. She shook her head, the gesture quick and short, but he knew what it meant. Most of the bullied didn't want to be dragged into the spotlight. Not 'till they were ready to tell someone.

"You're going to stick us together?" He scoffed, changing the course of what his words was going to say in a breath. "It's probably just going to lead to him opening his stupid mouth and saying something that pisses me off."

"You seem to be under the ridiculous idea that Mr. Donoghue is also receiving detention, Mr. San Román."

Asa's eyes narrowed into slits. "I wasn't fighting with air, Cromwell! He was in it as much as I was. In fact, he initiated it—"

"Enough!" she snapped. "You're not in detention for the fight, Mr. San Román. You're in detention because you were mouthing off at the disciplinary head and implying that she is an ape."

Asa knew—he really did—that he needed to shut his mouth. But when did he ever stop himself?

"Honestly, Cromwell. If I knew your feelings got hurt so easily," he said, grinning at the woman, "I can assure you I think you're prettier than an ape, if that is any consolation."

And Asa earned himself an extra week of detention.

If you enjoyed this sample, look for
Through Your Eyes
on Amazon.

ACKNOWLEDGEMENTS

Thank you to all my readers for their undying support, my roommates for embarrassingly spreading the word about this book, and my parents for raising such a bookworm.

AUTHOR'S NOTE

Thank you so much for reading *How to Save a Bad Boy*! I can't express how grateful I am for reading something that was once just a thought inside my head.

Please feel free to send me an email. Just know that my publisher filters these emails. Good news is always welcome.
kairy_aguayo@awesomeauthors.org

I'd love to hear your thoughts on the book. Please leave a review on Amazon or Goodreads because I just love reading your comments and getting to know you!

Can't wait to hear from you!

Kairy Aguayo

ABOUT THE AUTHOR

Kairy Aguayo grew up in a small town in South Texas. Her love for literature started on the online platform Wattpad and she has spent most of her time writing goofy novels. Her goal when writing is to make the book relatable and real, hoping to make it as uncliche as possible. Currently, Kairy Aguayo attends the University of Texas at Rio Grande Valley and hopes to entertain and help them get lost in her work.

Printed in Great Britain
by Amazon